Allan C McLean

And Delilah

THE CHINA RUN

"*The China Run* has that same disarming simplicity that you find in Defoe, and the same triumph by means of artless detail."
                                        H. E. Bates

"Told to perfection . . . the combination of excitement and sympathy gives it a most unusual flavour."   *Eric Linklater*

"Admirably told and wonderfully amusing.   I only wish it had been longer."   *W. Somerset Maugham*

BEHOLD THY DAUGHTER

"A magnificent story, destined to the widest popularity. *Behold Thy Daughter* is going to find countless readers.   It is the book of the month, and for that matter the novel of the year. It has humanity, robust good sense, excitement and fun."
            Malcolm Thompson, in the "Evening Standard"

"A substantial and satisfying novel, this.   Like a strong flowing tide, it surges forward; there is no resisting it. *Behold Thy Daughter* has enough action and atmosphere and a sufficiency of characters to stock half-a-dozen run-of-the-mill 'literary' novels.   Its vitality is abounding."
                    Daniel George, in the "Bookman"

"A work of remarkable accomplishment . . . infectiously readable, warm, sensible, human, and distinguished by a peculiar but most attractive humour.   Far too exciting a human narrative to be missed."
                    C. P. Snow, in the "Sunday Times"

"A rich book, packed with events.   Mr. Paterson . . . writes admirably, with vigour, precision, and a Defoe-like simplicity: and he has the saving grace of humour.   This is the most distinguished Book Society choice that it has been my fortune to meet for a long time."
            Morchard Bishop, in "John O'London's Weekly"

NEIL PATERSON

And Delilah

NINE STORIES

HODDER & STOUGHTON

The characters in these stories are entirely imaginary.

FIRST PRINTED 1951

PRINTED AND BOUND IN ENGLAND
FOR HODDER AND STOUGHTON LTD BY
HAZELL WATSON AND VINEY LTD
AYLESBURY AND LONDON

TO
SOMERSET MAUGHAM

CONTENTS

CONTENTS

THE LIFE AND
DEATH OF GEORGE WILSON

who was an Extraordinary Fine Specimen

IT WAS MADAME GOLLATZ WHO BROUGHT IT ALL BACK TO ME. She came into the office sideways, being the only way she could get through the door, eased herself on to the chair that I had had specially strengthened for her, and sat panting and nodding and smiling till she had enough breath to speak. Then she said: "Did you see about the Princess Circassy?"

I hadn't, and I said so.

"She died. It was in the Sunday paper. Aged twenty-nine. That kind don't live long, do they?"

"No," I said. Ma Gollatz is thirty-six stones and only sixty-one inches high, and as a rule her kind do not live long either, but I did not think of that at the time, because of course I was thinking only of George; and Ma knew that, and began a fine chatter of words to make me think of other things.

"And the second George?" she said. "Well, well, the *lieb-chen*. What news do you have of the little man, I wonder?"

"My boy? Oh, he's fine. He's doing pretty good at this new school I sent him to. Do you know what it costs me a year?"

"Yes, you told me, Joe. It must be a very high-tone establishment."

"The best," I said. "The best. Nothing but the best is good enough for young George. He is going to be a doctor, you know."

"Yes, I know. Old Max and me, we are very proud of it. We have all come a long way, Joe."

I looked round the office. I could see my name on the frosted glass door. "J. Harrap & Co., Entertainments." It had an important look. "Yes, I suppose we have," I said. "Did it say anything else in the paper about the Princess Circassy?"

"No, just that she was dead. It didn't even give her measurements."

"Well, that's the way it goes," I said. I drew a couple of lines on my account-sheet, and when I looked up I saw that Ma was crying.

"George was a great gentleman, though undersized," she said. The tears were sliding along the creases in her cheeks. There was nobody had tears like Ma for size, and she cried easy of course, like most of these fat ones. "Been thinking of him all day. I can't get him out of my mind. Wasn't he a great little gentleman, Joe?"

"He was all that," I said.

2

I bought George Wilson in 1928. I bought him from old Sol Goldstein, who was in the same line of business as me, although at that time Sol's side-shows were of a higher class than mine, Sol being established, and long past one-night stands. I knew that Sol would sell George to me, because Sol was beholden to my Dad, and Sol never forgot a favour nor an insult, though he paid both in his own time and in his own way, and he did not like to be rushed. If I had asked for George Wilson I would not have got him. I asked for the lightweight out of the boxing booth.

Sol raised his hands and screamed at me. That boy was the best he'd got. That boy meant the difference between life and death to Sol Goldstein. Without that boy Sol Goldstein would starve.

I thought for a bit and tried again. "The indiarubber man," I said.

"My God," Sol said. "Hark at him now! The indiarubber man. Do you know what I pay that indiarubber man in wage! More then your ha'penny shows draw in a month. Look, Joe, it's you I think of when I refuse. Can Joe afford it, I say to myself? Can he support the burden? A thousand times no. With a show like yours you cannot carry the expense of them important artistes. Be reasonable, Joe. Be prudent. Now, was there anything else you saw?"

"No, Sol, there was nothing else," I said. I got up like I was going. "I don't mind telling you I'm disappointed, because I need new blood, and need it bad, and if I don't get it now it's curtains for the Harrap shows."

"To tell you the truth," Sol said, "as I would tell it only to the son of your father, I cannot afford to give you the Murder Kid or the Rubber Man, and that is the honest truth of the matter, Joe."

I reckoned that I could have them if I wanted them. But I didn't want them. I wanted George Wilson. I had wanted him from the first time that I saw him. I put my hand on the doorknob.

"Wait, Joe," Sol said.

"All right, Sol," I said. "Let's see what else you have. How about? . . . No. I'll tell you what, Sol. I don't much want him, but I'm willing to take the midge, provided you let me have him cheap."

"He's a great artist, that midge," Sol said. "Frankly, I would not like to part with that midge. Just listen, Joe."

I had to listen to the list of things the midge could do. He could walk the trapeze. He could sing and dance. He could swim. He had a good memory. He could learn a part. He could even read and write and he lived clean. He was no trouble. Any showman that had that midge had gold in his hands.

"I'd rather have the fighter," I said.

"All right, Joe," Sol said. "How much you bid?"

"For the fighter?"

"For the midge."

"Ten pounds."

We talked for the rest of the morning, and in the end I got George Wilson for twenty-eight guineas. He was cheap at the price, and I was very pleased about it. I knew it was one of my best bargains.

3

I have seen a lot of midges in this business, but I have never seen one like George Wilson. The fact is, there is something wrong with most midges. Sometimes it is their heads. Sometimes it is inside their heads. Sometimes it is their bodies. Their heads are too big for their bodies or their bodies are too big for their legs, or their voices, if they have voices, aren't like the voices of human beings at all. You might think that a midge was like you and me, only on a small scale, but, bar one, I never saw any midge like that, that was just right, good-looking in the face and with small perfect bones and all its muscles working and its actions natural and no loose flesh round its neck. I never saw one like that yet except for just this one midge George Wilson that I'm telling you about. Mind you,

I'm not saying that George was perfect, because he wasn't. George had faults like anybody else.

At the time I bought George he was twenty-eight inches high and weighed nineteen pounds. This was because he was out of condition. He wasn't being given enough exercise. He wasn't being watched, and all the time he was supposed to be taking his exercise he was sitting around studying for some examination at London University. Can you beat that! A midge studying out of books sent him by a university. Nobody would credit it that didn't know George, but that was the kind of midge he was. Different. Just plumb different.

He told me about it the first day. "I want to be frank with you," he said. "This thing is important to me. I must have a degree of privacy."

And then he told me about this university business.

I suppose I must have gaped at him with my mouth open.

"I don't want to be forced into evasion and disloyalties," he said. "I want to be perfectly honest with you."

I noticed that he was pale and that his hands were trembling, and I guessed that he was frightened for all his fine manner, and I spoke up to him like he was a person. "That's okay with me," I said. "I suppose a midge has a right to a private life like anybody else." I thought about that after I heard my voice saying it, and I reckoned it was fair enough, although it was not a point that had struck me before. "Provided," I added, "you don't stray out of your compound, of course."

Looking back, it seems crazy that I ever thought of keeping George in a compound, but you have to remember that when I first got him I did not understand George very well and he did not understand me either.

Take that first day when we got to the station, for instance.

"Where's the shawl?" George said.

"What shawl?" I asked.

"For wrapping me in. Aren't you going to pretend I'm a baby?"

"Hell, no," I said.

"Pity," George said. "I much prefer the shawl to the basket. The shawl is *infra dig.*, but the basket is dehumanising and also damned uncomfortable. I see you haven't got a basket. You're not going to put me in that attaché-case, are you?"

"I'm not going to put you in anything," I said.

"Then you'll have to pay for me."

"I'll get you for a half."

"My God," George said, grinning. "Don't tell me there's a man in your trade with morals!"

I didn't want any cracks from him or anybody else about my morals, and I told him so. "Everything's on the up and up in my stalls," I said, "as you'll find out for yourself, and I don't hold for no looseness any more than my father did before me."

I got him through for a half.

"What's your age?" I asked in the train.

"Eighteen."

"I thought you were older. That's what Sol said. That you were eighteen. Are you really only eighteen?"

"Yes," he said. "I don't tell lies."

I looked at him and knew he was speaking the truth.

"And you, Mr. Harrap? How old are you, if I may ask?"

"I'm twenty-five."

"You look younger, you know."

That got me on the raw. After all, I had been through a lot, and I was sole proprietor of Harrap's Side-shows and Stalls. I was a man of substance and I owned several people. I was touchy about looking so young. I had, I remember, even grown a moustache to look older. I was pretty foolish in these days.

"Personally, Mr. Harrap," George said, "I should have put you at about twenty-one."

"Well, I'm twenty-five," I snapped, "and *I* don't tell lies either."

"I believe you," George said. He sat looking up at me for a long time, then he said: "You know, I think you and I have struck rather lucky in each other."

Until you got used to George he knocked the breath out of you.

"What do you think, Mr. Harrap?"

"I think you talk too much," I said.

4

The spring I got George I was working in with J. V. Green. It was his fair, and I hired the space off him for my tents, and when he moved on I moved too. I had four shows at this time, five if you count the coco-nut shy. The shows were Madame Gollatz, the Fattest Woman in the World, Max Brown (Ma Gollatz's husband) and his performing fleas, Vendini the Strong Man, and the boxing booth with two pugs, both old. I was working very close to the bone. I remember I was so hard up that I had to offer Madame Gollatz and Max as securities to Entertainments Ltd., before I could get the new stuff I needed for George. Anyway, after a lot of letters and paper-signing, I got the gear, and I set George up in the new tent as King Minos VII, the Smallest Man in the World. He did a five-minute work-out on his trapeze, his tight-rope act, and a trick-cycle stunt, and you could shake hands with him as you filed out at tuppence a time. The weather was good that year and I did all right, and George was a success. I paid off my debts, including the one to Entertainments Ltd., and hired a new tent and platform and scenery, and started a ventriloquist act, in which I had George dressed up in a doll's mask with a flap lip and a jointed wooden suit that covered him completely, including his hands and feet, and by the end of autumn this act was doing so good that I raised the price from threepence to sixpence and was still packed out, most performances.

In the winter I got an offer to put the act on the stage, but I turned it down, because I did not see any future in it, and then at Christmas time I hired George out at great profit to play a character known as Tinker Bell in a London show called *Peter Pan*; his name was in the papers, and I got an offer for him from a London theatrical agent. It was a good offer. It was a mighty good offer when you think what I paid for him—£250. And I think he would have gone to three hundred.

I spoke to George about it. By this time George was living in my room and calling me Joe and going everywhere with me.

"What do you think, George?" I said. "It's a good offer and I'll give you a decent split."

"If you need the money, Joe."

"It's not a matter of needing the money. It's just good business. I'll give you a fair share."

"I don't care about the money, Joe."

"For Pete's sake," I said. "If you don't care about money, what do you care about?"

George just looked at me. I can see him now—his mouth opening to say something and then closing tight and his face getting red, and his eyes—those small grey steady eyes of his—hooked right into mine. He was sitting on the edge of the table with the white silk rope across his knees. He had these ropes fixed all over the place so that he could climb on to anything without being helped. He had his hands clenched on the rope, and I saw the whites of his knuckles, and I got angry and shouted at him. "You'll never amount to anything if you don't care for money," I said. "The sooner you start caring about money the better, my lad, see!"

"All right, Joe," George said. "I will, I'll start caring."

I didn't like the quiet way he said it.

"After all, business is business," I said.

"It's all right, Joe. I understand. When'll I have to go?"

"Go where?"

"To London."

"You're not going to London," I said. "Two hundred and fifty pounds is chicken-feed. I'll get a lot more than that for you yet."

I never talked or thought of parting with George again. I never even told him of the offers I got. As far as I was concerned he was off the market. It just wouldn't have been good business to sell him. He was worth too much to me.

The next year I got three new fighters, and I started a Hall of Mirrors and two shooting galleries. It was about this time that I first began to have money in the bank, but I never left it there long. I used it to buy up new acts and new stalls. I had one idea only. To expand. To have a fair of my own. To be the boss.

George had given up the university business.

"I don't need it now," he said. "I'm fulfilling myself. The old show business is good enough for you and me, Joe."

"You're damned tootin, pardner!" I would say.

I was on the way up then. Nothing could stop me. I had spent my life in the business, and I knew all the people that counted. I always got on well with everybody, and even men I didn't know trusted me because I was Honest Joe Harrap's son, and around this time it seemed that everybody was falling over everybody else to put something good my way. I was always travelling, always buying, always working. George worked hard too. He was interested in everything about the business, and he had a kind of gift for it. I talked my deals over with him and I listened to what he had to say. He became my right-hand man, and when I went to look over a turn or a site I used to leave him in charge and he would run the show and be the boss for maybe two or three days at a stretch. The queer thing was that nobody ever tried to make a monkey out of him.

"He's got dignity," Madame Gollatz used to say, winking and wheezing and smiling. "Dignified, that's what he is. The little one."

Maybe that was it. Maybe it was because of this dignity of his that nobody teased George. I don't know. I do know that George could speak for me to everybody, and they would do just like it was me talking, that is, all except Vendini the Strong Man.

Vendini and George never struck it off. Vendini had the strength and the brain of an ox, and he could not get it into his skull that George was a person. He used to follow George around just to stare and laugh at him. He did not mean any harm. He liked George, but the way he liked George was the way Max liked his fleas and he never got wise to the fact that George did not like him or that George had feelings.

"You clod!" I've heard George say. "I have more matter in my little finger than you have in your whole body!"

"Listen!" Vendini would say, delighted. "Listen to 'm talking! The words!"

"You big ape, what does size count! You may not know it, but the greatest men who've ever lived have been little men. Take Napoleon."

"Mother o' God, listen! Just listen. Such speech! Say more, dwarf. The words that he has, in a voice!"

I think George hated Vendini. He used to say that he didn't

care what Vendini said or did. Vendini was a moron, beneath a man's notice, but I think that Vendini always hurt him very much and that really he hated Vendini.

I tried to explain George to Vendini myself, but he could not understand that it hurt George to be treated like a freak out of business hours; he just could not understand that George was human.

"I say sorry," Vendini said, nodding. "You get him. I say sorry now." And he began to laugh again, just thinking of George, looking at the bottom of the door where George would appear. "You get him. I say sorry. Yes. Ha, ha, ha!"

It was hopeless.

5

I remember it was soon after George's twenty-first birthday that I took him to see the Princess Circassy. I had found her some months before when I was in Newcastle to sign up a middle-weight, and I had it all fixed with Iggy Pullitzer who owned her that if George liked her he would sell for £100. The Princess Circassy couldn't do much—she was just an exhibit—and she wasn't worth £100 or anything like it to me; but I didn't mind spending the money if it made George happy. I didn't tell George what we were going to see, I wanted it to be a surprise to him, but I wired Iggy Pullitzer that we were coming and to have the Princess all primed up.

Well, it wasn't a success.

The Princess Circassy was the prettiest female midge I ever did see—she was only one inch taller than George—and she looked just fine when you saw her by herself, but alongside George she had a kind of coarse look, and I knew right off that they'd never make a match of it.

"Hiya, big boy," the Princess Circassy said, looking George over.

"Gives you a turn, don't it," Iggy said, "to hear them midges talkin' up like folks! B'jeez, if they ain't just a pair now!"

"C'mon in," the Princess Circassy said to George, standing at the door of her compound and touching her hair with her hand. "We can be kinda private in here. C'mon, big boy."

"No, thanks," George said.

"The little runt's scared," Iggy said, laughing. "Go on you, George! Go on, Lofty. Go to it!"

I knew I had made a bad mistake. I got George away as quickly as I could. I reckon I felt almost as bad about it as he did himself. I didn't know where to look.

"I'm sorry, George," I said.

"It's okay, Joe."

"I meant it for the best. I didn't know it would be like that."

"It's okay. I understand, Joe."

We didn't say much in the train. George was white as a sheet, and I hadn't any use for myself and didn't want to hear my voice talking.

"Joe," George said after a long time.

"Yes, George."

"Did you see that place she lived? It was no better than a . . . manger. And, Joe—she smelled! Did you notice?"

"Yes, George," I said, though I hadn't noticed. "I'm sorry. I'll make it up to you."

"It's all right, Joe."

We never spoke of it again, but later that night, after we got home and George was turning in—he needed a lot of sleep: twelve hours was his usual—he said something to me that I never forgot. "Joe," he said, "do you know something? I hate midgets."

6

The following year George took ill with the 'flu, and I thought that I would lose him. I got three doctors in. The doctors said positively there was nothing any of the others could do that they each of them couldn't do on his own, but I reckoned there was bound to be one of them smarter than the others, same as in any kind of business, and I wanted only the best for George. Two days and two nights I never left his bed, and then, on the morning of the third day, his temperature went down, they said he was out of danger, and he started moving his lips to speak.

"I'm sorry to be such a trouble, Joe," he said.

"You shut up," I said. "You lie quiet like the nurse says, or I'll tan the hide off you." I had a temperature myself then and I could of wept like a woman, I was so relieved. After all, midgets that are a commercial proposition like George do not grow on trees.

When he was better I sent him down to Eastbourne with Max Brown to take a holiday and get strong. He didn't want to go. He argued this and that. You never heard such arguing. He kept on at it. His place was with me, he said.

"Listen," I said; "what kind of mug am I and what kind of master-mind are you that I cannot get on very well without you for a bit! You'll do what you're damn well told."

"All right, Joe," George said at last. "I'll go. But you'll send for me if you want me, won't you?"

"I won't want you," I said.

I missed him though. The place was kind of empty and the evenings seemed long with nobody to tell about the day's work and nobody to help count the money. I looked forward to his letters—he wrote every day—and I spent time fixing up some gadgets that I knew he would like, including a little rope ladder up to the safe in the wall which nobody had ever touched before except me.

Max and George were to stay in Eastbourne for three weeks but before the end of the third week I got a letter from George that ended:

"*Will you please come down, Joe? There is somebody that I want you to see. It is very important, so please come, Joe. Max will add something to this letter too.*"

Max had added:

"Yes, you better come, Joe."

I went down to Eastbourne the next day. I couldn't think who it was that George wanted me to see, and of course I never guessed the truth.

Max got in a word to me at the station. "It's a girl, Joe," he said, behind his hand. But even then I didn't cotton on.

They took me to see her that evening. She was working behind the bar in the *Duke of Buccleugh*, a house that the police have now closed. She had a white face and very black hair, and she was about eighteen years old. Her name was Mary Guiseppi.

"Well, there she is," George said. He kept glancing at me nervously, waiting for me to speak. "Isn't she beautiful, Joe?"

"I'll not deny it," I said. I watched her. I could see she was ill-treated like George had said. It was in her manner all the time, and when the woman in the black dress, the manager's wife, spoke to her, her eyes turned over like a frightened darkie's. She was scared all right, and she was moreover not a girl who knew her way around. It was plain that she had not been in the trade for long, because when the men at the bar laughed out loud, teasing her, she got red in the face and acted kind of paralysed. I was not impressed.

"Beautiful maybe," I said. "But dumb."

"You should hear her sing, Joe," George said. "One night, when there was hardly anybody in and the manager's wife was at the pictures, she sang to us. She has a wonderful voice, hasn't she, Max?"

"She sings real pretty," Max said. Max never took sides. "Yes, sir, real pretty, Joe."

"She's got talent," George said. "She's just what we want, Joe, isn't she? The glamour angle. I knew you would see that. Wait till Joe sees her, I said to Max. Joe can spot talent a mile off. Joe is the greatest discoverer of talent in the business. . . ."

"All right, George," I said. "All right, take it easy. You can't talk me into buying something I don't want, and I don't want that girl, and that's final."

"You don't understand, Joe," George said. He started to tell me all over again how badly she was treated, and then he stopped suddenly, his body stiffened, and his face set like a mask, and he said in a new hard voice: "Look! There he is. The manager."

The manager was a little man with a waxed moustache. He had a part in the story George had been telling me about this girl Mary Guiseppi. It was the usual part. Middle-aged man, ageing wife, pretty young girl. You know the kind of thing. And the wife knowing it too and knocking sweet hell out of the girl.

"Joe, she's got nowhere at all to go, and nobody in the world, and she's good, Joe, and sweet, and she has a beautiful voice. She really has. Listen, Joe, she's got glamour. She's what we need. She would brighten up any act."

"Be reasonable, George," I said. "What could I use a girl like that for?"

"For nearly anything."

23

"For instance?"

He thought about that. "Well, at least she could work in with the fleas. Please, Joe, listen to me. . . ."

"Sit down, George," Max said. "Everybody's looking at you."

George got down off the table. He had got so excited that he had climbed up in order to look me in the eyes. He was very pale, and I guessed he had not yet got over being ill. He was trembling.

"Please, Joe," he said. "To please me!"

"No," I said.

"Joe, I'll never ask you anything else. . . ."

"No," I said. "For the last time. No."

The rest of the night I hardly got a word out of him and the next day it was the same. I didn't like the look of him, and I wanted to get a doctor.

"There's nothing wrong with me," he said.

"Sulking, are you, then?"

"I'm not meaning to, Joe."

I stayed on another day because I was worried about him, and he saw that, and tried to be cheerful, and that was worse than if he'd just sulked. At night I heard him tossing and turning in his bed, and in the morning I knew that he had not slept.

Max puffed away at his pipe and read the paper like it was none of his business and he didn't care anyway. "I reckon he's pining away," he said. "Yes, sir, I reckon his little heart's broke."

I stood it till dinner-time, and then I lost my rag watching George pick at his food, pretending to eat.

"Oh, for God's sake!" I said. "All right, I give in. I'll take your girl."

Max was smiling as if he had known all along that this would happen.

"On one condition only," I snapped. "Provided I get her cheap."

7

Everybody thought it was very funny, George having a girl. I must say I thought it a pretty good joke myself, at first, and one way or another George had to put up with a lot of chaff and sniggering that was meant kindly enough, but which must have hurt him considerably, as I realised later.

The girl Mary Guiseppi was no trouble to anybody. Ma Gollatz took her into her tent—Ma was too big for a caravan, and she and Max did not live together, although they were as devoted a couple as ever I saw—and Mary acted as a kind of housekeeper to Ma and made herself useful doing odd jobs about the stalls. I was busy—I was expanding all this time—and I might have entirely forgotten the girl if George hadn't kept harping on about giving her a chance.

George had taken to books again, and any time he wasn't rehearsing or doing a job for me you'd find him in a partitioned-off corner of Ma Gollatz's tent poring over books with Mary Guiseppi.

"All she needs is polish," he said. "You wait. She'll be a great lady one day. A great star. You'll see, Joe."

After George had been on at me for about a month I asked Max Brown how he would feel if the girl sang outside his fleas. Max didn't stand on his dignity. He said he would feel fine, he didn't see what harm it could do, and neither did I, and so it was fixed that Mary Guiseppi would do a short number to draw the crowd before each of Max's shows. We threw up a platform, and George used his own money to hire a micro-phone and buy some of the latest records.

Mary herself came to thank me.

"It's George you want to thank," I said.

"I know. But I wanted to thank you too."

I asked her how she was getting on. Was she settling down all right?

"Oh yes," she said. "I'm the happiest I've ever been in my life. I'm very, very happy, Mr. Harrap."

She was too. You could see it shining out of her, and it puzzled me, because I couldn't think for the life of me what she had to be so happy about.

Well, Max's takings got good. They got better than they had ever been before, and I started paying Mary a wage, and I bought her a couple of dresses and sent her into town to have a good doing over at a beauty place, hair and nails and all that, and George was on top of the world, and strutted about like a cocky boxer, saying, I told you so.

I do not think that I ever regarded Mary Guiseppi as a good proposition, however, until I teamed her up with Gaspar and Lily Freud, the lions. It was George that gave me the idea, saying that Lily appreciated Mary's singing, she was always quiet when Mary was singing, and when Mary spoke to her she would scratch her ears on the bars of the cage and do a kind of soft growl. I had seen this happen before, a lion cottoning on to a person for no special reason that you could see, and this time it gave me the idea for the Singing Beauty and the Beasts turn that I later showed in all parts of the civilised world.

George did not like the idea of Mary going into the cage with the lions. He did not like it at all at first, and Signor Blanchino (Jack Evans, the trainer) and me had to talk him into it. It was quite safe. Gaspar and Lily were circus lions of the third generation, and there was no viciousness in them, although Lily got kind of contrary at times. But, as I say, she started off liking Mary, and she soon got wise to the set-up, namely, that she got fed after Mary finished singing and she didn't get fed at all if she hollered. That year I raised Mary's wage three times and George started calling it her salary.

At first I had it figured out that George would get over the craze he had for this Mary Guiseppi. I thought that George had just too much intelligence to let himself fall seriously for a full-sized girl, but I am wiser now, and I know that intelligence does not count much in a man where women are concerned. Anyway, George got worse. They called him Mary's lamb. He followed her everywhere, and he talked about nothing else. She was never out of his mind and hardly ever out of his mouth. It was Mary this and Mary that till you were sick to the teeth of it. At first when she did her turn with the lions he got so white you would have thought there wasn't a thimbleful of blood in his whole body, and though later he got used to the act, he never liked it, and was always in a blue funk when Mary was in the cage. If ever a man was crazy about a girl, that man was George.

It was only after Mary joined us that I began to notice how touchy George was about his size. He was always telling you about little men. Napoleon and Nelson and J. M. Barrie—it was J. M. Barrie who wrote the play *Peter Pan* that George did so good in—and Lloyd George and Louis XIV, a foreign king that invented Louis heels, and many other characters out of history that I had never heard of. According to George, they were all little men and he kept telling you about them. He got Bill Dekker, the carpenter, to build him a rack for stretching exercises and he sent secretly for booklets on How to be Six Feet Tall. He got thin and pinched-looking, and I did not like it because he had started on a trapeze act with the Stein Brothers in which, hanging by their legs, they tossed him to and fro like a ball, George turning a somersault in mid-air in the finale. He needed all his strength and his wits for a dangerous stunt like that, and I finally told him I wasn't going to stand for any more nonsense. I told him he had to give up stretching himself on this rack of Bill Dekker's.

"All right, Joe," he said. "Anyway, it was a mistake. I have been thinking a great deal about it, and I have come to the conclusion that the physical side of things is not important to Mary. For instance, it never occurs to you that I'm a midget, does it, Joe? I mean, you regard me as just a normal human being, don't you?"

I nodded.

"Well, it's the same with Mary. As a matter of fact, I don't think she's the physical type at all."

"She looks physical enough to me," I said.

"That's because you don't know the side of her that I know. You don't know the real Mary, Joe. It's things of the mind— yes, and of the spirit, that interest Mary, Joe."

"Maybe you're right, George," I said. But I did not think he was. It had seemed to me that I had a problem on my hands with Mary Guiseppi. Now that she was well-fed and no longer scared, she was getting to be a good-looking girl. She was shining with health; she had that kind of ripe look you see in girls that need marrying off, and a lot of the men around the place were watching her. But naturally I didn't want to say anything about that to George.

"In eighteen months' time," George said, "I should have five hundred pounds saved. That's a lot of money, Joe."

I waited. I knew there was more to come, and I knew it was something unusual from the way George was flipping and scratching at the pages of his book. I could not see his face, but his neck was red. He said in an ordinary voice: "I'm going to ask her to marry me then."

I knew that I was the only person he would tell, that he was trying the idea out on me, and I made my voice as ordinary as his.

"That'll be fine, George," I said.

I didn't like it at all, but I reckoned a lot could happen in eighteen months.

One of the things that happened was that I got robbed. It was at the time of the first of my big deals. I was buying up Solomon's show, lock, stock and barrel. Seven thousand quids' worth. I drew the money from the bank in the morning, put it in the safe in the caravan, and left George in charge while I went uptown to the lawyer's office where Solomon had said to meet him. We sat all day getting the paper work squared up, and then we went across the road to an hotel for a drink, and the lawyer bought an evening paper, and there was the story on the front page.

ROBBERY AT HARRAP'S SHOWGROUND

We read it.

"Bad luck, Joe," they said.

"This is not bad luck, Solly," I said. "This is the end of Joe Harrap."

On the way back to the ground I read the report half a dozen times. George had been assaulted, the safe forced, and a considerable sum of money stolen! The police wished to interrogate a man in connection with the affair. This man was known, the paper said, as Henry Spicer, showman, and it gave his description.

Harry the Spice! He was no showman. He was a roundabout engineer. He had been with me two years, and I had always thought he was a steady kind of chap. Seven thousand quid—most of it borrowed on security—plus the week's takings, plus the week's wages. Harry the Spice had made a pretty job out of me. I was finished with a capital F.

George wasn't in the caravan and nobody knew where he was. Nobody knew anything. They were all calling me Mr. Harrap now. When I was alone I put my head down on my arms on the table and cried.

Freddy, the Kid from the Boxing Booth, came in without knocking and said: "Do you know what? Harry the Spice ran off with old Dave Green's daughter well as your dough. The youngest." He stood with his hands in his pockets smiling at me. He was after Mary Guiseppi, and she had told him where to get off, but he hadn't, and George and me had had to tell him too. He hated the lot of us. "The old Spice, eh!" he said, laughing.

"Get the hell out of here," I said.

George came in then.

"Where the hell have you been?" I shouted.

George didn't say anything. He reached up and laid an envelope on the table.

"Answer me! Where have you been, you miserable little runt?" I said, and I hit him on the side of the head with my open hand. George went down like a clay duck and lay on the floor at my feet staring up at me with an awful look on his face.

"You damned useless pigmy!" I said.

He pulled himself up then and scuttled out like a rat.

After a long time I saw the envelope and opened it. There were four cheques inside, all payable to Mr. Joseph Harrap: £200 from Max Brown, £100 from Hermione Gollatz,

£75 from Mary Guiseppi, and £407 15s. 6d. from George Wilson.

Even his shillings and pence. His last bit.

I went out after him. I went out running. Folks who heard me calling George thought I had gone off my head.

I asked Mary.

"No, Joe," she said. "I haven't seen him at all. I'm sorry about the money, Joe."

"That doesn't matter now," I said.

I searched the whole ground. I tried all his usual places first and then I tried every place I could think of. There was no sign of him at all, and nobody had seen him.

"I ain't seen him since the afternoon," Ma Gollatz said. "He called a meeting. You should of heard him speak, Joe. 'Joe's always done right by us,' he said. 'Joe is the finest man in the world. He'd never let any of youse down if you was in a jam.' You should just of heard him. My, he had the tears pouring down my cheeks. Didn't he speak good, Max?"

"Eloquent," Max said. "Eloquent indeed."

"We gave all we could, Joe."

"You won't be sorry," I said. "When I get on my feet there'll be bonuses for all of you, you Max and you Ma and Mary and George, and I'm doubling all your wages as from now. Only for Pete's sake let's find George."

When it got too dark to look for him any longer I went back to the caravan, and there he was in bed, undressed, with his eyes closed, pretending to be asleep. He wouldn't let me say I was sorry and he wouldn't let me thank him. He wanted the whole thing forgotten.

"After all, we're partners, Joe," he said.

I told him about doubling the wages. I thought that would please him, but it didn't. He said I paid them all plenty. He said it wasn't good business. But he was wrong there, of course, though I couldn't get him to admit it. Good friends are always worth good money, and something more besides.

Later I asked him where he had been. "I looked everywhere for you," I said. "Where were you, George?"

"Underneath," he said, pointing.

"I don't understand."

"I was underneath the caravan."

I stared at him. "That's a hell of a place to go."

"It's private," George said.

In the middle of the night I was wakened by the police hammering on the door. They had caught Harry the Spice, and they thought that I would be glad to know that they had recovered the money. They were quite right, of course. I was very glad.

8

Soon afterwards I started in Big Top. This had been my father's ambition before me, and I wished he could of been there the night I opened Harrap's Continental Circus, featuring an Amazing Collection of World-famous Artistes and Savage Beasts, a Thousand Thrills and a Thousand Laughs. George and me moved into a new big caravan coated all over in a highly artistic way with gilt, and we gave a party to all the old hands, including Mary Guiseppi, to celebrate our success. The takings went from good to better. In the trade they said I had the golden touch, and it was around this time they started calling me Lucky Joe Harrap. Myself, I think Hard-working Joe Harrap would have been a better name, because I never had my nose off the grindstone, but I'll not deny that I did have luck.

It never struck me now that there was anything funny about

George's craze for Mary. I thought about it often, but I could not find a way to stop George from being hurt and hurt bad. For all his size he had the biggest heart I ever saw in any man, and there was a fair chance that Mary Guiseppi would break his heart, and if George's heart broke there was more than a fair chance that he would die. It wasn't very funny. Mary Guiseppi meant the whole world to him, and he showed it in a hundred ways every day of his life.

I soon reckoned that George had more than his £500 saved and I kept expecting the fireworks to start. I watched them both, but George was the same as always, and it wasn't him but Mary Guiseppi who began to act like she was under a strain. George noticed, of course. George always noticed everything about Mary, and he came to me about it. He said she was working too hard. He said he thought she was scared of the lions. He said she needed a holiday. He asked me to have a talk with her.

"And, Joe," he said, "maybe at the same time you could sound her out about me, eh?"

"What do you mean?"

"About marrying me."

I didn't like it at all.

"I would be extremely obliged to you, Joe." You should of seen his serious face. "Please, Joe."

"Oh, all right," I said at last.

I spoke to Mary Guiseppi. I beat all around the bush and didn't say much as first. She looked ill. She had a white face at the best of times, and now there were blue shadows under her eyes and her breasts kept heaving all the time she spoke. She had kind of noticeable breasts.

"There's only one thing wrong with me, Joe," she said. "I want a change."

"Maybe we could arrange a holiday."

"No, Joe, I want more than a holiday. I want to leave."

"Quit, you mean!"

"Yes. Quit," she said.

I didn't need to think about that. Mary Guiseppi was one of my best acts. She was worth money to me, and I didn't want to lose her, and besides, there was George to consider.

"Is it money?" I asked.

"No."

"You won't get better money anywhere, you know. You won't get as good."

"It's not money."

"What is it, then?"

"It's just that I want a change, Joe. You know how it is."

"I don't know how it is. People that work for me just don't walk out on me." I hesitated. I was so sharp around this time that I could of caught a weasel asleep, and I had a sudden hunch of the thing that was troubling her. It was George, of course. She was tired of seeing George on the door-step. He had got on her nerves. I had never thought of her angle before, but I thought of it now, and I saw it might not be very nice for a normal dumb sort of girl to be courted by a midget. I asked her point-blank. "George couldn't be getting on your nerves, could he?" I said.

"No, of course not. I like George."

"George loves you."

"And I love George. I think he's wonderful. You know that, Joe."

"Yes, yes," I said. "But what I want to know is, do you love George the way a woman loves a man?"

I saw the colour rush up her throat to her cheeks, but I was paying more attention to getting the words out than anything

34

else. I wanted to clear up this thing once and for all and I said bluntly: "Would you marry him?"

She jerked her arm as if she was going to strike me, but her hand finished up on her throat. "That's a pretty bloody rotten thing to say, Joe Harrap!" she said, eyes blazing, and flew out of the door. George hadn't quite finished making a lady of her, you see.

I'd made a mess of it. I scratched my head and tried to think what I had said to make her fly off the handle. It wasn't like her. She was usually such a good-natured girl and, though she was a pretty singer, she had never come over temperamental before. In the end I sent for Ma Gollatz, because I reckoned Ma was sure to know what the trouble was.

I told her what had happened.

"What's wrong, Ma?" I said. "Why has she been off her stroke these past months? Why does she want to leave?"

Ma held up her hands and spoke the foreign way she always does when she gets angry. "Clever the word for you is," she said. "You make money. You understand reading and writing. You fill the big tent with people. Oh, clever the word for you is, Joe Harrap. Extreme clever."

"Oh, come off it, Ma," I said. "I'm not so clever, and you know it."

"No, you are a great fool. The girl is in love with you. Simply, that is all."

I couldn't believe my ears.

"But, Ma," I said. "Ma, she's George's girl. George loves her."

"So do you," Ma said. "You are really a great fool, Joe, although the boss."

35

9

I didn't sleep much that night.

A few days later George came to me and told me he'd asked Mary to marry him, and though she hadn't said yes she hadn't exactly said no. The way George spoke I reckoned Mary had said no all right, but she'd wrapped it up so soft he'd never felt it hit him. George was full of hope. I put my head down on my arms on the table so that he couldn't see my face.

"What's wrong?"

"I'm thinking," I said. "There must be some way out of this."

"If you would speak to her again, Joe."

"You think I can fix pretty near anything, don't you?"

"Pretty near, Joe," George said.

Well, I spoke to Mary. I went into the tent and gave Ma the thumb and she cleared out. Mary was sitting by the door darning stockings. She had on a blue shiny frock and she looked very pretty. I cleared my throat.

"Listen," I said. "Ma says you're in love with me."

"Yes, Joe." She never even looked up from her darning.

"Ma says you're in love with me too."

"Well, that's right. I reckon I am."

"Oh, Joe!" she said, and her face was beautiful. She came and put her arms round me and her body pressed everywhere against mine and I shook like a frightened foal.

"I don't know much about this kind of thing, Mary," I said. "I wouldn't fool you. I've always been too busy."

"Oh, Joe, you're so beautiful," she said. "And I love you so much. I've always loved you. Put your arms round me, darling." And she began to cry. She was shaking just the same as me.

After that I couldn't face George, and that was why I went up to Liverpool next day to look over a couple of acts I had had in mind since the previous winter.

"You'll write, won't you, Joe?" George asked before I left. He always asked me that. "Even if it's only a post-card."

"Sure I'll write, George," I said.

I had planned to stay away for a week. Mary and I talked it over, and we reckoned a week would be long enough for us to find some way of breaking the news to George.

"It's got to be some way that won't hurt him, Mary," I said.

"I wouldn't hurt George. You know that, Joe. I wouldn't hurt him for anything. But there must be some way, and we'll find it between us."

Well, I didn't find a way, and I knew that I never would. There are times when thinking just does not help, and this was one of them. George reckoned Mary was his girl. You couldn't think past that, and after three days I gave up trying. I couldn't stay away from Mary any longer. I went back.

I took the morning train from Liverpool and was in London in the afternoon. I had to wait for a connection, and I did not get to the town where we were pitched till after the show had begun.

The clowns were in the ring and the Stein Brothers, trapezists, were just running in to take their first bow when I arrived. I couldn't see Mary, and I waited for a minute, watching, to get the laugh that always came when Stefan Stein took George out of the pocket of his big coat.

Whenever I saw George I knew that there was something wrong. At first I thought it was the make-up, but when I saw him do his preliminary work-out I knew it was more than that. I had a kind of premonition then.

"My God, something's going to happen," I said.

Mary had heard that I was back, and the next thing I knew she was tugging at my sleeve.

"Well, hullo," she said. I didn't hear the rest.

"There's something wrong with George," I said.

"I've fixed all that," Mary said. "That's what I'm telling you, darling. Do come and see." She kept pulling at me, and I wanted to look at her, but couldn't take my eyes off George. "In Ma's tent," she said. "Come on, Joe. You've seen this act a hundred times before."

Gee, she was pretty! We held hands going across the Common, and she asked me if I had missed her and I told her I had, and for a few minutes I forgot all about George. Then the tightness came back to my stomach.

"You haven't done anything to hurt George, have you, Mary?"

She laughed at me. Course she hadn't, she said. But she had fixed everything. She had had a brainwave and fixed everything, and now she just couldn't wait for me to see. She was giggly with happiness.

We went into Ma's tent. It was dark inside.

"Yoo-hoo, where are you?" Mary said.

Something moved in the back of the tent, and I had to jerk my eyes down to see what it was.

"Hiya, big boy," the Princess Circassy said.

I stared at her. Mary was watching me, smiling. "Well, what do you think of her? Isn't she wonderful, Joe? She's George's. I bought her for George, and he's crazy about her. . . ."

I didn't listen to what she was saying. I was thinking of a day several years ago, and I was hearing George's voice. "She smelled, Joe," George was saying. And then: "Joe, do you know something? I hate midgets."

"Well, say something, Joe!" Mary demanded. "Don't you think she's wonderful?"

"Oh, my God!"

"What's the big idea! Who are you my Godding at?" the Princess Circassy said.

I turned on my heel and started to run back towards the Big Top, but I knew all along that I wouldn't be in time. I heard the scream from a hundred voices and I heard the music stop. When I got there they were carrying something into the dressing tent and I knew it was George. There was a doctor with them.

I pushed my way to the front.

"Will he live, doctor?" I said. "You! Doctor!"

"Back's broken," the doctor said.

George opened his eyes and looked at me then. "Hullo, Joe," he said.

"George," I said. I couldn't say anything more, and when he smiled I couldn't even look at him.

"Don't take it so hard, Joe," he said.

Mary was beside me now, and she was crying without trying to hide it and Stefan Stein was crying with great dry sobs in his brother's arms at the back of the tent. It was Stefan who had dropped him, although it wasn't Stefan's fault, of course.

"Do you know what she did, Joe?" George said. "She gave the Princess Circassy four hundred pounds. Every penny she had. All her savings. She did that for me, Joe."

I stared at him.

"Imagine her doing that for me, Joe. She must have loved me in a sort of way, mustn't she, Joe?"

"Of course I love you," Mary said, crying.

"Only a few minutes now," the doctor said.

"He'll want to see the Princess Circassy," Mary said. "You want to see the Princess, don't you, George?"

39

"Yes."

"Come on, Joe," Mary said to me. "He'll want to be alone with her."

"No, no!" I said. I tried to explain. "It's us that George wants. We're his people."

"I want the Princess Circassy," George said. "Mary's quite right. Leave us alone together."

"George," I said.

Mary took my arm.

"Take care of her, Joe," George said.

I nodded. I couldn't speak.

"We'll both take care of her, George," Mary said. She thought George was speaking about the Princess. She didn't understand at all.

I couldn't take my eyes off George.

"George," I said.

He just smiled at me.

"Oh, come on, Joe," Mary said, crying. She pulled me out of the tent. "Where is she? Oh, there you are. Quick!" she said to the Princess Circassy. "He wants to see you."

I lifted the Princess Circassy off the barrel that somebody had put her on because she was nervous about being left on the ground alone since a pony had trampled on her, and gave her a push towards the tent. She took a couple of steps and looked round doubtfully, and Mary said, "Go on," and she went in, walking very slowly.

Mary hid her face in my chest, and after a minute I put my arms round her and held her. There was no use blaming her. She didn't know what she had done, and I would see to it that she never did know. That was the way George wanted it. That was the thing he had been saying to me.

"They were in love, Joe," she said. "It was love at first sight.

You should of seen how pleased George was. Oh, poor, poor George!"

I held her very tight and stroked her hair. I made my voice come. "It's all right, baby," I said. "It's all right."

Later, I tried to settle up with the doctor. He wouldn't take anything, but he kept talking. He had never had his hands on a midget before. He had found it very interesting, he said.

"Amazing, you know," he said. "Turned his head away when his girl came in. And she wouldn't go near him. No human feelings at all. I suppose they're all like that, aren't they?"

I would have liked to of told him, but I couldn't. I could only look at George.

The doctor pulled on his gloves and nodded at the table.

"Extraordinary fine specimen, though," he said.

AND DELILAH

I CAME ACROSS THE CARD WHILE I WAS CLEARING OLD LETTERS out of my bureau prior to getting married. It was a small, gilt-edged business card, and printed on it in discreet pica was the following inscription:

"Sr. Tomás Sansón
A. and J. Garcias, Exporters of Finest Amontillado Jerez
Representative in Portugal,
15, Rua Nova do Corpo Santo, Lisbon."

Sansón! I could not place him. Tomás Sansón. Had I bought sherry from him? The name said nothing at all to me, and it was not till I had fingered the card for some minutes that the vague outline of a man took shape in my mind's eye. "Of course," I said, and then, as I stared at the card, recalling the details of that odd incident, the illumination came, and I began to chuckle and then to laugh. I couldn't stop. I put my head down on my arms and laughed till I was sore. I understood it all now, and it seemed incredible that I had not seen the point, this superbly ironical point, before.

45

It started with my slapping a Nazi Consul. That sounds like an interesting story, but it is not at all interesting. I slapped him because I happened upon him at a time when he richly deserved to be slapped, and on behalf of a lady. My action was disinterested. I did not know the lady, and I must confess that when I slapped the Consul I did not know he was either a Nazi or a Consul, although it would not have made any difference, I would have slapped him anyway.

At the time it was not fashionable to slap Nazis, and of course there were immediate repercussions. But I had better begin at the beginning.

This all took place in Estoril, back in 1938. I was living in the Hôtel Splendide as a guest of the management, who, having read some of my bull-fighting stuff, and having been impressed, I presume, by the exaggerated tributes of the literary critic of the *Portuguese Telegrapho*, had commissioned me to write a handbook on the Costa do Sol, a sort of glorified brochure to tempt the English to the Sunny Coast of Portugal, and in particular—provided they had enough money—to that Millionaires' Home-from-home, Europe's *de luxe*, Most Ultra-modern, Sumptuously Palatial Hotel, the Splendide. You must pardon the capital letters. It was, of course, that kind of brochure.

As a matter of fact, Estoril can stand a few capitals. It is situated about twenty kilometres from Lisbon, and it is a truly beautiful little town, lying snugly in the narrow plain between the Sierras and the sea. It is full of colour. The pink and white houses tiled in polychrome and Dutch faience blue delight you with their pastel-coloured shutters and their window-boxes teeming with geraniums that bloom all the year round. The stores, quaint and characterful—many of them are built in the Moorish tradition—are aglitter with every kind of Portuguese filigree work, and as you stroll through them the salesmen do not pester you. There is colour everywhere. The smooth, sandy beaches are overgrown with expanding noon flowers that carpet the rocks and dunes with immense patches of purple and red and yellow, and in the gardens that border the blue Tagus there is always a riot of flaming cactus. The roads are of an impeccable, a Persil white, and along them, threading their way through ass-drawn wagons with home-made wheels, drive Hispanos and Mercédès-Benzs carrying beautiful, bejewelled women to assignations at the Casino and the Termas, or luxury spa; and along these same gleaming roads the knife-grinder, piping shrilly, trundles his china-riveting and blade-sharpening apparatus, and the *varinas*, or fishwives, come from the fish-market at Cascais wearing the shoes and stockings that the Government has now decreed that they must, lest you think Portugal a backward country, and walking with a stilted self-consciousness that contrasts oddly (or did then) with the assurance of their voices singing their wares: "*Ameijoas, cockles epolvos, octopus* !"

I enjoyed Estoril. I even enjoyed writing about it. I liked the sober, diligent, black-clad Portuguese whom God, with a smile, had planted in these flamboyant surroundings, and I liked the admirable blend of vulgarity with good taste which you see everywhere and which is the essence of Estoril. I was temporarily one of the very idle rich myself, and the fat men with beautifully manicured hands did not offend me. I was grateful to them for providing me with the spectacle of their sleek, gleaming, chromium-plated cars and their equally sleek kept women, and I used to sit by the hour on the terrace that overlooks the absurdly formal gardens of the Casino sipping from a glass of *fundador* while I contemplated the human panorama (of legs mainly) and listened with a minimum of malice to every conversation that I could hear.

It was the finest holiday I had ever had, and I was in no hurry to end it. I wrote only in the period between my *cha* (after-siesta tea) and dinner, and I had, if I remember rightly, finished only half my booklet when the lady, regrettably, appealed to my finer if somewhat dormant instincts, and I coshed the Consul.

Well, of course, there was a high old hullabaloo. The following morning I was paid the full amount specified in my contract and asked to leave the hotel within twenty-four hours, this latitude deriving from the management's knowledge that I had a case against them if I cared to press it. But I didn't want any more fuss. I agreed to leave, and it was on the evening of the same day—my last in Estoril—that the incident which I am going to tell you about took place.

Everybody in the hotel knew of the strong-arm affair, of course, and everybody was talking about it. The Consul, it appeared, was cordially disliked, and I was peppered with congratulations. My progress through the foyer was like a triumphal march. I was the local lion, and quite briefly, for the spell of this one evening, enjoyed all the advantages of notoriety. Make no mistake about it, there are advantages to notoriety, one of them being, I found, that members of the opposite sex whom you have admired but who certainly have not noticed you now noticeably admire you.

I had danced a couple of times with the girl in the green frock before we got down to essentials. She was Spanish, of course, and had that slightly Spanish smell, but I cannot think of anything else that I would have liked to change about her. She was tall, up to my nose, had black hair and blue eyes—she was from the north. She told me the name of the town, but I have forgotten—and, dancing, she had the grace and the power of a black panther. I had seen her once before, and had been

48

impressed by the poise of her head, an insolence somehow, and the speculative rake of her eyes as she paused on that occasion at the door of the cocktail bar. I had thought her a lulu, a title which I do not readily confer, and now, after dancing with her a couple of times, I knew that I had been perfectly right: she was all of a lulu, and I do not mean anything derogatory by that. Madeleine, whom I am going to marry, is also a lulu.

"Lisa," I said in Spanish, "let's go out."

She gave me a look which titillated my spine, although it was not the sort of look that usually passes between the sexes. It was impersonal, and comprehending.

"Come on," I said. "Let's get some air."

"All right, but it is necessary for me to be wrapped."

"I have my car."

"Good. But I nevertheless require a wrap."

She put her head against my cheek and we drifted over to the doorway. "Wait for me in the bar," she said. "I wish also to repair my toilet, but it will not be of long duration. Wait at the end of the bar where you can view the staircase, and when I descend I shall make a sign to you. Is it clearly understood, darling?"

"It is clearly understood," I said. "I shall await you with a conflagration in my veins."

It is possible to say that sort of thing in Spanish. As a matter of fact, it is almost impossible not to.

"I shall return with all velocity," the girl said. She gave me a warm flick of her eyes and went up the staircase. I stood watching her legs going away from me. They were firm and naked, and looked very brown against her flickering white underskirt. Her shoes also were white and the heels were noticeably large. I remember thinking, absurdly, that they had a kind of brutal look.

I went into the cocktail bar at the near side of the dance-floor, ordered a Martel, and leaned back against the crescent-shaped counter, where I had an excellent view of the dance-floor and of the staircase beyond.

It was there that I was joined by the gentleman whose card I was to find in my bureau.

2

I was accustomed on this particular day to the attentions of strangers, and I did not specially notice the little man when he offered me a drink. I barely glanced at him throughout our entire conversation, because I was busy watching the stairs for my lulu, and now I can remember only that he was small, that he had a nondescript, clean-shaven face, that he was dressed in the faultless black of the business-man, and that his voice was crisp and slightly Castilian. I might not recognise him if I saw him again; yet I remember, I think, every word of our conversation from the time he caught my interest by mentioning Pedro Gonzalez.

"You must beware," he said, "of the fate that befell Pedro Gonzalez." Prior to this he had been congratulating me on my Spanish novels, one of which he had read, and on my bull-fighting articles. "I presume you have heard of Gonzalez, of course?"

"Of course," I said. "I suppose he is the most notorious matador of modern times."

"Notorious," my friend said. "Yes, it is so. And once, only a fraction of time ago, he was famous, with a glory and a dignity unequalled in Spain. Now he has only the fame of disrepute. He is notorious. You must beware, *m'amigo Ingleez*, lest your life continue the parallel, for you must know that Pedro Gonzalez also struck a Fascist, and also for honour."

"A Nazi?"

"To be precise, a Falangist. But the distinction is too subtle for observance. A horn will still gore, though you call it by a flattering appellation. Nazi, Fascist, Falangist. It is not of consequence. But you have heard this, I have no doubt, of Gonzalez?"

"I have not heard it, Señor," I said. "I have read only of the incident of the *coleta*, when the Madrid crowd expressed their disapprobation, and those who had worn his favours were beaten in the streets. For the rest, I have heard but rumour."

"You never saw him run the bulls?"

"Never," I said. "I regret it."

"He was an artist," the little man said. "A great artist. The last of the classicists. He did not run bulls for a living like those commercials you see in the ring today. He did not care for money. He lived only for his art and for the artist's glory. He aspired to bring the running of bulls to perfection. He was imperturbable in this design. Señor, you are an enthusiast, a real *aficionado*, and I contend that it would have given you much pleasure to have witnessed his cape-work, his classical passes, his *recorte*, his *veronica*, so pure and stylised, the bull and the *muleta* and the man in a single mould, the movement of incomparable fluidity yet with the air of great simplicity that belongs only to the master like Belmonte, like Gonzalez."

"I gather," I said, "that you were acquainted with Gonzalez."

"It is conceded, Señor. Permit me to effect an introduction. My card. Yes, I knew Pedro Gonzalez with intimacy. I knew him before he was married. Then he was at the summit of his achievement. He was celibate as a priest. He neither smoked nor

drank. He lived entirely within the limits prescribed by training and—I make my joke—although a Castilian, in this period
of his life he smiled freely. Then on tour, in Pamplona in
Navarra, he met Tisbea, who was of humble origin, but young
and excessively beautiful. Tisbea married him. I reverse the
natural order by design, for assuredly, although later he conceived a great passion for Tisbea, in the beginning it was she
who desired and married him. I personally am of the opinion
that she loved him truly at this juncture. She was very proud
of her husband—of his rectitude, his art, his fame. You must
understand that Tisbea, although unfinished in education, was
possessed of considerable talent, and thus in a brief period of
time acquired gentility from the men and women of lustre in
Pedro's society. Her tastes, which had hitherto been simple,
developed into the tastes of a woman of fashion, and soon she
no longer strove to attain the level of Pedro but rather to
elevate him to her successive planes. At times she would manifest the symptoms of jealousy—there was no other woman:
that would have been an absurdity. No, it was in the bulls that
she recognised her rivals. She spied on his training, regarding
the various acts of discipline as the rituals of a fetish from which
she was for ever excluded. She created scenes. 'You love
your stupid bulls,' she would say, 'better than me.' And then
when Pedro denied it she would demand proof. She would
require him to break training and accompany her to a theatre
or a function. Sometimes Pedro withstood her, but not always.
He had no experience in the management of women. He
tolerated her jealousy, and he tolerated also her acquisition of
new, sophisticated friends, men equally with women, with
whom he had no acquaintance. Tisbea's scenes became more
frequent, and of increasing violence. I trust, Señor, that you do
not find this preliminary account of negative interest?"

"It is of great interest," I said, and I meant it. I had always wanted to know more of Pedro Gonzalez, the idol of Madrid who had committed the only sin that the bull fans will never forgive: turned coward; and who in the moment of his humiliation had been exposed as a charlatan and a liar in the trifling but dramatic matter of his much-publicised *coleta* or pigtail. I kept my eyes on the staircase. I wanted to hear the whole story, but I also wanted to see the girl who had stepped so providentially into my arms, and I wanted this more. I wanted to be reassured of her reality. I found her more interesting than any story, and I had to master a quite unreasonable irritation with the little man for distracting me from my own thoughts. "Forgive me if I give the impression of inattention," I said. "But I am expecting a friend. Meantime, permit me, Señor, to replenish your glass. And please continue."

"I shall relate the facts of the *coleta* incident. This is a veracious account, but it is not to be recorded. At the time of this affair Pedro's fame was at white heat. A documentary film of his life had been made and distributed all over Spain. You saw it everywhere, although of course you cannot see it now because it has been withdrawn by official decree. In this film mention was made of the *coleta*, and it was exhibited with considerable magnification, Pedro turning his head from left to right to display it. You will have learned perhaps that he, Pedro Gonzalez, alone of all the modern *torreros* retained the *coleta*. Naturally every *torrero* must wear the *coleta* during the *Corrida* when he is actually running the bulls, but it must be understood that this *coleta* is nowadays an object of artificiality appended to the back of the *torrero's* head. The *coleta* is traditional, and Pedro Gonzalez was superbly a traditionalist and a classicist. He alone of all the *torreros* grew his own hair into the shape of a *coleta*. It was a symbol."

53

"But surely," I said, "it was proved that Gonzalez's *coleta* was a sham!"

"Let me continue, Señor. Pedro Gonzalez's *coleta* was of the hair of his head, as I shall presently make manifest to you. This *coleta* was a symbol to him. It was a symbol equally to the tens of thousands of *aficionados* and—in a converse manner—to Tisbea, his wife. In Pedro the pigtail of the bullfighter was a source of humiliation to Tisbea. She spoke of it with scorn and on numerous occasions. It was the mark of his trade. It was a conspicuous emblem which attracted attention, and in the cafés even foreigners from the luxury hotels would remark it and make Pedro the focus of their curiosity. Such attention did not displease him, for he knew it to have a basis in respect, and he accepted it as a tribute to his profession and to his personal art. But Tisbea disliked it exceedingly. She hated the *coleta*. It was her enemy. On an occasion she adjoined the table of two young American women of sophistication and wealth who had witnessed a performance of Pedro in the ring and who now, inspecting him, spoke in the way that women will always speak, assessing the *torrero*, not as an artist, but as a male animal, ignoring totally the subtler mechanics of the performance and concerned only with the incidental embroidery. 'His sash,' they said. 'Those scarlet pants. The marvellous brocaded tunic. My dear!' they said, 'do you remember the ripple of the muscles on his forearm? So primitive.' You know the way these women speak, Señor. And then one said to the other—I translate freely—'Darling, how would you like to be embraced by a man with a pigtail?' and the other said, 'It would be rather revolting, don't you think? But it would excite.' And they surveyed Pedro, noting his points, like buyers considering a young bull in the corral. That night when Tisbea returned from a party at which there had been much champagne, she found Pedro asleep, in which state he had been confirmed for some hours, being due to run the bulls in a charity nocturnal the following evening. Thereupon Tisbea extracted the pearl-studded razor from his toilet-case and cut off his *coleta* close to the scalp. Pedro wakened while she was bending over him, and in the struggle for possession of the razor the open blade slashed his wrist, severing the radial artery, so that a spout of blood several feet in height issued forthwith. Pedro removed the trousers of his pyjamas to stanch the wound and a tourniquet was applied with all haste.

"The next day the arm was stiff, but he could employ it. The fingers, however, were powerless. 'The cloak can be attached to the leather strap on my wrist.' Pedro said. 'In this way it will be possible for me to function in the *Corrida*.'

" 'It is impossible,' they said. They tried in vain to dissuade him. 'It is suicidal,' they said. 'It is madness.'

" 'It is imperative,' Pedro said. They could do nothing against his iron resolve. For him it was a matter of honour. The tickets for the Plaza had already been sold, and a lottery as to the split second of the minute in which he would kill had been organised in national proportions. Had he met with an accident of the nature that may befall a man of honour, it is possible that they might have prevailed upon him to default, but he was determined that not even the humblest spectators in the *Sol* should suffer the smallest diminution of entertainment by reason of his wife's indiscretion, and in such matters of the profession his word was law. A *coleta* of the correct hue and texture was obtained with difficulty, for it must be understood that this is not commonly an article to be purchased ready-made, and he left the hotel in good time to be dressed in the punctilious fashion that his prestige demanded. The rest, Señor, is common knowledge. He was weak and lacked agility. The crowd was very patient, but you know the bull crowd. They do not make allowances, and from the great *torrero* they demand perfection. They hate an act of cowardice, yet they seek it always as hounds seek a scent, and having once sensed it in a falter or a compromised movement they are immediately in full cry. They had loved Pedro and he was their idol. Now they pelted the arena with cushions, with bread, with bottles. They stood and screamed in a hysteria of abuse.

"Pedro could not kill. The picadors did what they could, but he was very weak and his hand would not grasp the sword. It was a matter of universal relief when, finally, the horn pierced the ribs under his left arm, and the tragedy was brought to a conclusion. Momentarily there was a revulsion of feeling. The great Gonzalez was down with the horn in his breast, and the bull, sluggish now but still on the move, was scuffing his weighted horn across the sand of the arena. There must be an explanation, it was thought. Then someone saw the *coleta*, and the cry went up. 'His *coleta*! Witness it, the great *coleta*!' It became the universal shout. '*Coleta*, *coleta*! The great *coleta*!' You will understand that the *coleta* had become detached from Pedro's head. The hoof of the bull was caught in the elastic band of the *coleta*, and as the bull dragged his hooves along the arena he dragged also the *coleta*, and emphasis was laid thus upon its artificiality, and those leaning over the *barrera* could see plainly the elastic. It was the final insult. They had been proud of the classical *coleta* of Pedro Gonzalez. It had been a symbol of honour and now was the symbol of his degradation, and of their degradation also as his dupes. They would not forgive that. They reviled him, and in fact I am assured that even today, Señor, they spit on his name in Madrid. I trust that I retain your interest?"

"You have undoubtedly the whole of my attention," I said.

"Save only the courtesy of my eyes. You have presented this history with commendable clarity and provided the food for much thought."

"There is more. Pedro Gonzalez lay in the infirmary for many weeks. He was sorely *cogida*, and they said that he would have died had it not been for the ministrations of his wife Tisbea. She made a residence of his bedside. She attended personally to all his requirements. She gave him strength and heart. She was beyond praise, but while still convalescent Pedro learned that she had contracted the habit of unfaithfulness with the Senior Consultant Physician. Although unrecovered in health Pedro, like you, Señor, struck down the traitor, who was a party man, a Falangist, of note. He struck him down with his fist, and killed him."

"Killed him!" I said incredulously.

"It was a matter of honour. There was a knife in his fist. He then confronted Tisbea with the act. 'That restores a semblance of cleanliness,' he said.

" 'You fool!' Tisbea said, laughing in hysteria. 'You would have to kill the half of Madrid!' It was thus that Pedro first learned the character of his wife. You will understand naturally that it was now necessary for him to leave the country of his birth and to proceed with all despatch into exile, in which project he was assisted by a loyal friend, who procured for him a disguise and unauthorised documents."

"And Tisbea," I said. "What happened to Tisbea?"

"She was his wife, Señor, and accompanied him." He paused and raised his glass. I thought that the narrative had come to an end, but I was wrong. In a few seconds he continued, speaking more slowly now and choosing his words, I felt, with greater care. "The remainder of the facts, though less concrete and lacking, perhaps, a truly objective basis, serve to point the moral and may be welcome, accordingly. Now that Pedro was no longer of consequence, Tisbea's attitude was observed to change, and there was marked deterioration in their relations. She no longer treated him with the courtesy that the humblest man demands of his wife. She was cold and defied him in public. It is to be conceived that primarily Pedro believed this revulsion to be due to his act of vengeance, but with the passage of time it became clear that her distaste was not a physical affair, and indeed that what remained of her respect rested solely upon this same act of vengeance. She was gratified that he had killed for her: it was, conceivably, the thing about him which gratified her most. Manifestly, this is not a solid foundation for marital content, and soon there were other incidents of an unsavoury nature. These, fortunately, were brought to a termination by Pedro without further fatality, although in the case of one lover, blood, undoubtedly, was let. It is not my object to make a catalogue of infidelities. Such affairs are not of interest in themselves, Señor, but only in so far as they illustrate a peculiar facet of character, in this case, namely, that it was not the essence of Pedro or of this man or that which Tisbea admired, but rather his environment of glory. You may have noticed, Señor, that talent is no substitute for breeding in the assessment of matters of good taste, and thus in many instances, notably the affair of the barber of Vila Real, Tisbea confused the base alloy with the metal, and selected for association not a man of true fame, but a creature of notoriety whose name had been driven like froth to the surface of some seething cauldron of scandal. It was a source of regret to Pedro Gonzalez."

I liked that. And so did Señor Sansón. He repeated it. "Considerable regret," he said. "And to us, Señor, who are men of affairs, it is perhaps an oddity worth remarking that that which

his wife most hated in Pedro—his glamour, his glory as a
torrero—was plainly that which, in fact, had attracted and
bound her to him; and it is surely an oddity in which one can
see the hand of God that in cutting off his *coleta*, in humiliating
and ruining him, she condemned herself to the oblivion of exile,
and was thus by her own act bereft of that which she most
coveted. But we can leave such talk to the moralists. I am a
practical man, Señor, and my concern is with practical affairs.
I perceive that your glass is empty."

"No more," I said. "I have had a sufficiency. There is just one
matter that now remains obscure to me. I accept your version,
Señor, of this history, but I do not understand why Pedro
Gonzalez should have retained so fickle and cruel a wife."

"It is possible that he still loved her."

"No, no," I said. "It is not possible, surely. And she. Why did
she not leave him? Why did they continue to live together? I
am a writer of fiction, Señor, yet with all the devices of my
trade I could not make such behaviour credible."

"Señor, is it not conceded that the behaviour of men is
seldom credible? It is possible that in her fashion she too loved.
You shrug? In such matters one cannot ever know. One may
probe the complex caverns of sex for a lifetime in search of
wisdom, and emerge a fool. I do not know the answers to your
questions. I do not know why they continue to live together.
But there is, surely, a factor of import which you have omitted
to consider. Consider it now, Señor. They were married."

This is the type of conversation which, crudely, is my cup of
tea. I was intensely interested now, not only in the story, but
also in Señor Sansón himself. I was interested in the man he had
revealed to me in his last few sentences, and I proceeded
immediately to develop a line of argument, for argument's
sake, to provoke contradiction and further to uncover the

texture of his mind. I was intent on this fascinating project, and had, for the moment, quite forgotten my date with Lisa when her voice sounded close to my ear.

"I am ready," she said. "I have been standing on the stairs."

"Oh, hullo !" I said. I swung round, and in doing so brought Lisa and Señor Sansón face to face.

"You !" Lisa said.

I realised immediately that some sort of *faux pas* had been committed, although I did not then realise its nature. Lisa was no longer smiling, and now, despite her recent repairs, she looked older and less extravagantly a lulu. Her face had become rigid : stylised, the alabaster mask of a sophisticated woman, the sort of thing you see hanging on beauty salon walls. It was a startling metamorphosis. I turned, for a clue, to the little man, and he gave me a small dismissive bow. He was unchanged— dapper, formal, and, above all, nondescript.

"Let us dance," he said to Lisa.

"I do not wish to dance. I am going out on the terrace with this *Ingleez*. Besides, you know how it always hurts your side to dance."

"Nevertheless, we shall dance, if you please."

"Very well, if you wish it."

He laid his hand on her arm, and she had to screw her head round to speak to me, her throat showing all of thirty and her eyes black and captive. "Darling," she said. "I shall come back. He does not understand it, in English."

I watched them go down to the dance-floor, then, because one must accept defeat philosophically in such affairs, I shrugged my shoulders, slipped the little man's card into my pocket, and turned to the bar. A Martel was clearly indicated. A big one.

As I sipped my brandy I found my eyes straying to the dance-floor. When I found them the girl was watching me above

Señor Sansón's shoulder while he moved her on implacably, dancing stiff-legged, yet with a certain formal grace, and the sudden thought struck me with an impact that drove the breath back into my body that he danced quite beautifully— like a bull-fighter, in fact—and that he was every inch a classi-cist, with a wound in his side to boot.

I left the bar without finishing my drink.

The following week I sailed from Lisbon, and of course I never saw either of them again. But from time to time at odd moments I have thought about them, and I have wondered whether my imagination, battening on coincidence, played me false or whether my Castilian friend really was Pedro Gonzalez. I have been confirmed in the one opinion and then in the other, but till now I have never been sure. I am quite sure now, how-ever, having his card before me and having at last observed its superb irony.

For Sansón, you must know, is the Spanish word for Samson.

SCOTCH SETTLEMENT

IT WAS HARRY GOT THE PICTURE. AT SCHOOL. THE EARTH was too hard to work in winter and so Harry was goin' to school, and big Andra Jamieson he had the picture, he was allowed books with pictures in his house, he had hundreds, he said, mebbe thousands, he had this picture down the leg of his pants and Harry said, "Give us it." Harry said he said, "Please, Andra." "You don't have to beg," Andra said. "It's yourn." And he gave Harry the picture, and Harry took me down past the clearing to the hemlocks and showed me.

"Mutts," I said.

"No," Harry said. "Dawgs. These are English setter dawgs and mighty rare. Real dawgs."

We looked at the picture. There was two dawgs. One was settin' on his backside and one was on his four legs. The one that was settin' was squintin' up at the one that was standin', an' he was tongue out and rarin' to go. I guess he was grinnin' straight at me. He was the dawg I liked the best of them.

"They're red dawgs," Harry said, "and their picture was took for sellin'. Anybody wants them dawgs he can have them, it says, for twenty-five dollars apiece."

"Is twenty-five dollars a deal of money, Harry?" I asked.

"Twenty-five dollars," Harry said. "Ah, yes."

We looked at the picture for a long time and Harry let me hold it.

"Ain't none of the kids in the whole of Canada belongs a pair of two dawgs like this," Harry said. "I aim to call mine Rover. What you goin' to call yours, Dave?"

"I was aimin' to call mine Rover too," I said.

We had a hide-out Harry built down there in the hemlocks at the edge of the water. There was no wet settin' on account of the canoe birch we laid down in strips for floor. We set on the floor of our own two's secret house and looked for a long, long time at the picture of the red dawgs. They sure was pretty.

"There's Gramma hollerin'," Harry said at last.

"I don't hear her."

"You never hear," Harry said. "Come on." He folded the picture and put it in his pocket, and we rolled up my trousers so as my gramma would not see the ends was wet and say, You been down by the hemlocks again, and then we went on up for our rations.

"Do you know where I aim to hide this picture?" Harry said.

"No," I said.

"In my grandaddy's boots."

I looked into Harry's eyes to see what he meant, and I saw that Harry meant what he said.

"But, Harry," I said. It was no use. Harry could speak faster'n me, and I never yet talked him into anything or out of any other thing. Harry was eight and smart, and I was but four.

"No other place," Harry said, his mind was made up. "Grandaddy's boots."

I thought of my grandaddy's boots and of my grandaddy. I had a bad stomach, thinkin'. "I wouldn't, Harry," I said.

"Safest place," Harry said. "My grandaddy has been to the Convention, and his boots is oiled and on the shelf. Come the spring, my grandaddy will put on his boots and go down to the Houses again, but till the spring there will be no comin' and goin' among people and no need for the boots, and no sich safe place in all the house as the insides of them. You take it from me, Dave," Harry said.

I shook my head. I didn't like it at all. I knew it was two sins. It was a sin to have a picture in the house, and it was a sin to touch my grandaddy's boots. My grandaddy was death on sin. He had eyes sharp as a woodcock for wrong-doin', and when he saw a sin he raised his voice to Heaven and said so, and if it was us had done the sins he took us into the wood-shed and beat us. Once he beat Harry justly till he bled. My grandaddy was a just and terrible man. He was bigger'n anybody's door I ever seen except our own, and he'd a bin bigger'n ourn too if it hadn't been he built the hole to fit hisself. He was thick as two towny men put together, and he had a black beard shaped like a spade that he could a dusted the crumbs off the table with by noddin' his head if he had had a mind to, which he hadn't. He could not write except for J. Mackenzie, his mark, and he could not read, only some capital letters and the names of God and Jesus and numbers up to 793, which is the end of the Bible, Amen, and he had not any yap like the village men but, Conventions, when he sat down Harry said the place where he sat became the top of the table and men pointed their talk at him and kept their traps shut when he opened his. He was a true Christian. He knew God's will, and wreaked it on us.

His boots was the best of all the things my grandaddy had, nobody had their like, they was fifteen years old, and he was famed for them. The folks down at the Houses had an idea he wore them boots every day of the year, and they rated him

high, Harry said, for this. Folks never guessed that he carried
the boots to the outside of the village and put them on behind a
tree. Folks did not know that when they came visitin', mebbe
once twice a year, my gramma spied them in the valley and beat
on the gong and my grandaddy would even come runnin' to get
shod before the company arrived. They was black beautiful
boots, none of us was ever let touch them, and there was Harry
aimin' to hide a picture in them, and pictures was agin God
and so was a finger on the boots, and my stomach was jest plain
draggin' itself up the track to our house.

My grandaddy was not in the house. You could kinda smell
when my grandaddy was in and when he wasn't, not sniff-sniff
with your nose, not that kind of a smell, but you could jest
smell the nice slack feel of the house.

"Where's my grandaddy?" Harry asked.

"Outside," my gramma said. "Now go and git washed, and
hurry, and Davy, you scour them hands. Harry, see he does
it."

We came in cleaned and knelt down at our chairs.

"Lord," Harry said, "Father chart hum hum bout to receive
hum hum blessed portion hum hum hummy umhum day and
night. Amen. Gramma, whereabouts outside is my grandaddy?"

"Amen, Davy!" my gramma said.

"Amen," I said.

"Is he in the wood-shed?" Harry said.

"Now pull your chair up afore you set on to it," my gramma
said to me. "And never mind the knife. Use that spoon. What
was it you was sayin', Harry?"

"I said, where's my grandaddy," Harry said.

"He's had *his* meat a half-hour," my gramma said.

"But where is he? Davy wants to speak to him."

"Me?" I said.

"Your grandaddy is out by the fallen tree," my gramma said. "He's amakin' of fish-hooks. Drink up your goat now, Davy."

"Davy aims to ask him for a dawg," Harry said.

I laid down my spoon and stared at Harry.

"Well, *I* asked last time," Harry said. "Of course, if you're feart to ask."

"I'm not feart," I said.

"Stop gabbin', Davy," my gramma said. "Jest let off gabbin' this instant and eat up your meat."

I ate up and drank my goat. My gramma was for ever pickin' on me, but she had only a little voice—she was small-sized—and meant no harm by it. Although she was small-sized, mind, she was clever. She could weave and, not only, she could read and write, and had spectacles to prove it. She did what my grandaddy said like the rest of us, but once when my grandaddy had me by the pants and there was high words flyin' round my ears, my gramma spoke a piece on her own, and that time it was my grandaddy did what *she* said.

"Gramma," I asked, "why won't Grandaddy let us git a dawg?"

"On account of its rations," my gramma said.

"We could git a little tiny dawg."

"It wouldn't eat but bucket scraps," my brother Harry said. "It would catch all the rats. It'll be a little white rattin' dawg, and we'll call it Rover."

"You'll hev to ask your grandaddy," my gramma said. She took the done dish off the table and went to scrape it in the backyard.

"You finished?" Harry asked.

"Near enough," I said.

"Lord," Harry said. I bowed my head. "Lord hum hum thank God. Amen. Amen, Dave!"

"Amen," I said. "Harry, I never yet seen a red dawg. Did you, Harry?"

"No," Harry said. "But them's red dawgs, sure enough. It says so in the writing. Now go on and git down to the tree and ask Grandaddy."

"Okay," I said. "You comin'?"

"No," Harry said.

I went half across the clearing, then I stopped and looked back. "What'll I say, Harry?" I asked.

"Jest say you want a dawg. Go on. There's nothing to be scared of."

When I had gone a little farther Harry shouted, "If he won't let us git a dawg, try him for some other kind of crittur."

"What other kind of crittur?" I asked.

"Any kind," Harry said. It was nothing to him. He was kicking stones round the front door, his hands in his pockets. "Hurry up," he said.

My grandaddy had a fire lit down by the tree. He had got horses' nails off old Neil Munro in the spring, they was the best and softest iron, and my grandaddy knew a way to burn them nails and make them into a steel bar, and then when he had filed a hook on the end of the bar he cut it off, heated it red-hot and tossed it in a bucket of water, and then he picked the hook out of the water and laid it on a hot iron till it was bright blue, and to finish off he dropped it in a fishin'-can full of candle grease, and it got black then, and when it got black it was finished. It was the best and strongest hook you ever seen.

When I got down to the tree my grandaddy was jest cuttin' a hook off the bar. He had his back to me and I could not see, but I knew that was what he was doin' on account of his arm went in and out like a saw. I thought I would wait till he finished cuttin', so I waited. I walked up close, and waited till

70

the hook fell off the bar. My grandaddy had tongs, and he took the hook in the tongs and put it in the fire.

"Grandaddy," I said, "Harry and me wants a dawg."

My grandaddy twisted the hook in the flames and laid it in a red nest in the fire. He had a very black face with the beard, but not his eyes, they was blue and dug right into you.

"Jest even a little mutt," I said.

"What do you want a dawg for?" my grandaddy said.

I could not tell. I knew that we wanted a dawg better nor anything, but I could not jest think what we wanted it for.

"A dawg is no use," my grandaddy said. "You can't eat a dawg."

I could not think of anything to say. I waited a bit, but there was no more talk from him and nothing more comin' from me, and so I went away.

Harry let off kickin' stones and came to meet me. "Well, let's hear it," he said. "What did he say?"

"Said no," I said. "Said you can't eat a dawg."

We walked round to the side of the house without speakin'. We heard my gramma come out the front and start hollerin'.

"Wants you," Harry said.

I looked at the sun. Was my bed-time.

"Harry, I want to be shook if I'm sleepin'," I said, "an' see them dawgs again. Will you, Harry?"

"All right," Harry said. He put up his hands for shoutin'. "He's comin', Gramma!"

I went round the front to my gramma.

"Davy," she said, "was it you hid the scrubber agin?"

I would have said no, but she had a hard face on. "I think it's settin' up there on the kitchen couples, Gramma," I said.

It was tub night. When I was in the tub I told her about my grandaddy. I told her my grandaddy was set agin a dawg.

"Gramma," I said, "I don't like my grandaddy."

"Hush," my gramma said. "Hush now, that's a terrible thing to say. Everybody likes their grandaddy."

"No," I said. "Gramma, Alec Stewart has a grandaddy is on his side."

"Is on his side?" my gramma said, and she left off with the towel.

"Is on his side," I said, noddin'. "Alec Stewart's grandaddy is. He told me."

"Your grandaddy sometimes does not always understand young uns," my gramma said, "and you are too small a young un to understand grandaddies." She rubbed the skin near off me. "Now get shirted up afore I lose patience, and take a great leap into the bed."

I got into the bed.

"If we had a little white rattin' dawg," I said, "it wouldn't eat but rats, and it could have a wee end offa my rations on the Sunday."

"Git over the bed," my gramma said, sharp, "and leave his room for Harry, and stop up all this gabbin' and git to sleep."

"All right. Good night, Gramma."

"You never can tell," my gramma said at the door. "You might git a dawg some day, Dave. Now git to sleep."

I lay waitin' for Harry.

I could hear next door. I heard my grandaddy come in and grunt, and I heard my gramma, her feet moved round the room, and then she spoke up to him.

"That dawg," she said. "The dawg that Davy wants."

I didn't ketch what my grandaddy said.

"You can't knock mansize sins outa boys that hasn't yit growed up to them," my gramma said. "Your own son's sons and you adenyin' them and drivin' them the same wrong road."

"It's God's road," my grandaddy said.

"It's a fool's road, James Mackenzie," my gramma said, "and it ends in cryin'."

Harry came in then, and there was no more talkin' save Harry, he had some gab, and my gramma said yis and no, and Harry came to bed. It was dark, and we couldn't see the picture, and Harry didn't want to talk. He said he was too damn bitter.

"If we *did* get a dawg," he said, "my grandaddy would only eat it."

I lay on my back for a long time. I heard my gramma and my grandaddy git into their bed and I jest lay on, thinkin'.

"Harry," I said. I kicked him. "Would he eat it skin an' all?"

"Eh?" Harry said, he was half asleep. "Eat what?"

"The dawg."

"I don't reckon my grandaddy is truly a dawg-eater," Harry said. "Good night."

"You don't reckon he would truly eat a dawg?"

"Not a whole dawg," Harry said. "Now shet up and go to sleep."

"All right, Harry," I said. "Good night."

2

I don't know if it was the next day or some other day, I think it was some other day, the men came to our house. They came ridin' on hosses, and you could see crowds more where they came from, they was without hosses and small as worms way down in the valley. The hosses dug in their heels by our door and the men hollered for my grandaddy.

My gramma put her hand up atop her eyes and took a good hard look at them.

"Where's Jim Mackenzie?" they said. The hosses danced.

"He might be fixin' the fence," my gramma said at last. "Up by the oats."

"Gee-up!" they said. "G'an!" And I ran out from the side of my gramma to watch them go. It sure was pretty to see them hosses calomphin' along, their hoofs hit sparks off the track and the men's backsides jogged up an' down.

"I reckon they came peaceable," my gramma said, "but it don't hurt to make sure. Davy, run down to the wood-pile and tell your grandaddy."

I told my grandaddy and he hit the axe blade into a hard-wood log and started for home, and I ran beside him.

"There was guns stuck on the hosses' necks," I said.

My gramma had my grandaddy's boots open for him at the door. "There was five of them, Jim," my gramma said. "One was Joe Cullis."

"Was the hosses sweatin'?" my grandaddy asked.

"No."

My grandaddy laced his boots and took his gun off the top of the door. I ran to git his cartridge belt.

"Thanks, Davy," he said.

We stood watchin' him till he hit the wood and we could not see him any more.

"Will my grandaddy be killin' the hosses too?" I asked.

"Your grandaddy's not agoin' to kill anything," my gramma said, "the idea." But she stayed at the door, listenin', and I was not sure. "You bide by the house now," she said. She took a last hard listen and went in through the door.

Soon I saw Harry, it was his time to be home from school. I gave the scalp whoop and ran across the clearing to meet him.

"Five hosses," I said. "Guns. Guns, Harry, and men ridin' fast."

"That's nothing," Harry said.

"They went calomphin' up to the oats and my grandaddy's git after them. One of the hosses was white."

"Nothin'," Harry said. "Nothin. Listen, where's grandaddy, did you say?"

"He went after the hosses. The hosses was . . ."

"And Gramma?"

"She's in. Harry, my grandaddy's booted up an' he's got his gun."

"Listen, will you," Harry said. "This is *important*. I got somethin' mighty special. You know what I got? Go on, ask me."

"What you got, Harry?" I asked.

"Not so loud," Harry said. "We'll jest ease down the hemlock way like we wasn't goin' nowhere in particler. Hisht now, I got somethin' you wouldn't guess. I got a babby."

"A babby!" I said. "A real babby?"

"Real enough," Harry said. "It's settin' on its hunkers in the hut chawin' away at a root. You feel the weight of it you'd know it was real. I've had it since the mornin'."

"Where'd you git it, Harry?" I asked.

"Found it."

"And is it really ourn?"

"It's mine," Harry said. "But you kin have a loan of it when I got other business. We kin run now."

We ran.

"It's declarin' again," Harry said. "Hear it?"

I heard it plain.

Harry ran on in front, and when I got to the hut he had the babby up in his arms. "Hisht now," he was sayin'. "It had lost its root," he said to me. The babby was dressed in a shawl and long pink pants. Harry set it down and it rolled over and howled. Harry set it up straight and held out the root, and it took the root and shet up and shoved it in its trap.

"Well, doggone," I said. "It's purely real."

"You kin feel it," Harry said, "if you crave to," so I felt it. The babby did not turn its head to look, but its eyes came round the side of the root and gave me a glower.

"Hullo, babby," I said.

It never said nothing.

"Kin it speak, Harry?"

"Ain't exactly gabby," Harry said.

"Is it new-born, mebbe?"

"No, no, it's gittin' on. Listen, Dave," Harry said, "you know what a babby needs best of all. It needs milk. So I aim to go an' tap the goat afore my gramma gits there, an' you bide, see, an' mind the babby. If it drops its root it'll holler, so give it its root back, an' if it still hollers sing to it."

"Okay, Harry," I said.

When Harry was gone I sat down beside the babby and looked at it, and it looked back at me.

"What's your name, babby?" I asked.

It never said nothing.

I poked round it with my finger to see was it well fattened up, and it was. I stroked the top of its head and it never moved, only its eyes, they squinted up; it was jest a young babby and did not know it could not see the top of its own head. It sooked hard at its root.

"Tomorra, babby," I said, "I'll cut you a hunk off the old hog. That's better nor root."

I thought I heard Harry, or mebbe it would be my grandaddy. I got a real skeer. I went out and poked my head round the side of the hut, and whenever I went away the babby let out a holler. "Wheesht!" I said. I could not see anything. I went back and said, "Wheesht now!" and when it saw me it stopped hollerin'. It had took a fancy to me. I went away some more times to see would it holler, and every time I went away sure enough it hollered and every time I went back it let off. I reckoned it was some birds I heard. I put my arms round the babby to lift. The babby was willin', but it was plumb solid. I got it up, but my legs had no notion to walk with it. I could of carried it fine on the flat, only them bits of canoe birch was not safe to walk on with a babby. "See," I said, "you're big as me now." I heard a curlew whistle and knew it was Harry, so I put the babby down quick and set it right way up, and Harry came in then. He had a half tin of goat.

"Take the root out of its mouth," he said, "and let me feed it."

I took the root out of the babby's mouth and the babby hollered. It wouldn't look at Harry's tin. It was its root it wanted.

"All right, give it the root to have in its hand," Harry said. He had that babby all weighed off. I gave it the root in its hand, and it shet right up and drank its milk, with Harry holdin' the tin and its face half inside of it.

I laughed to see it drink. "Sure has a thirst," I said.

"One thing about a babby," Harry said, "you got to wet its whistle near every hour of the day. My gramma near ketched me, Dave. I was jest finished at the goat when she came round the side of the house. Look now, you git up for your rations, it's near your time, in case she starts searchin' for you. I gotta wash up the babby an' do its chores."

"And then you'll take it up to the house?" I asked.

"No, no," Harry said. "I aim to keep it in the hut. There ain't nobody but you and me got to know about this babby. It's ourn."

I thought about that. That was good.

"Are we goin' to keep it for ever, Harry?"

"I don't know," Harry said. "We'll keep it here for a year or two anyways, till it's got a mind of its own, and then if it wants to hit the trail, won't be no stoppin' it. Now go on, Dave, up to the house."

I would of liked to bide and watch the baby git its wash, but I had to go for fear my gramma came down by the hemlocks, so I said good night to the babby and told it I would see it in the mornin', and went on up to the house.

The first thing I seen was my grandaddy's boots.

"Your grandaddy's at the water-shelf," my gramma said, "so say your prayers good."

I said my prayers and ate my rations and drank the wee drop milk that was all my gramma had gotten off the goat, then I said more good long prayers, then my grandaddy came in from the water-shelf and my gramma took me out and scrubbed my hands and face.

"Gramma," I said, "when I was a babby did I have a towel round my middle?"

"You did," my gramma said. "And all babbies has."

"Why?"

"Why?" my gramma said. "So as the babby is all plugged up, of course. A babby is like a cat, you see. It has got to be teched about sich things, jest like a cat or any other young critter."

"But it's better nor a cat," I said. "Nor a dawg neither."

"Granted," my gramma said. "Now say good night to your grandaddy and git bedded."

I said good night to my grandaddy and got into the bed. I clean forgot about the hosses and the guns, I was too busy thinkin' about the babby, the games me and it would play, and what we was goin' to call it, that specially.

When Harry came in I asked him.

"I ain't jest settled on a name yet," Harry said, he whispered. "You thought up somethin'?"

"We could call it Rover," I said.

"No, no."

"Rover's a good name, Harry," I said.

"Rover's a dawg's name," Harry said. "It's a good name for a dawg, but not for a babby. I had a notion now to call it George."

"George is a good name too," I admitted, "but I like Rover best."

"I tell you t'ain't fitten," Harry said. "And whose babby is this babby anyway?"

"It's your babby, Harry," I said.

"Well," Harry said, "I am goin' to call my babby George after the King, an' that is now its name, an' we will have no more argy-bargy outa you, Dave, that is if you crave to keep friendly with me and my babby."

"I think George is an extra good name, honest, Harry," I said.

We heard my grandaddy say his prayers through the door, and then we heard the bed creak, and we knew that him and her had gotten into it.

"Harry," I said, "how did you know about them wettin' cloths the babby has on round its middle?"

"I remember my mamma with you," Harry said. "I used to help her, and times I did you myself."

I thought about Harry doin' me. I couldn't remember, but Harry remembered near everything that ever happened from the start of him an' me. Harry remembered my daddy and my mamma. He used to tell me pictures of them in bed, and my daddy was a big man in a white shirt, as strong and thick as my grandaddy, but not so hairy and twice as clean, and my mamma was purely beautiful with a soft way of strokin' you and you could tell her anything, and she did a lot of laughin', but never at you, and her face was like in a picture book. Not like my gramma, who was kind, but her face was strictly useful. I asked my gramma about my mamma, but my gramma never liked to look back, she only said, "Your mamma was somethin' special, even if she did marry our Alec. Remember always she was somethin' special, puir lassie; she had hands fine as a lady's."

"What are ladies' hands like, Gramma?" I asked.

"Very clean," my gramma said.

I used to wash my hands sometimes when I was not told, because I wanted to be somethin' special too. I looked at my hands in the dark and I thought about the babby and the babby's hands. The babby's hands was fat and thick and dirty. "Did you wash the babby's hands, Harry?" I asked.

"Wheesht," Harry said. "Yis, I washed it all. I'm goin' now."

I must a been half asleep, lyin' there thinkin', because I saw that Harry was over by the windy and he was dressed with all his clothes on. "I'll be back afore they git up in the mornin'," Harry said, and he climbed right out the windy.

I listened for a long time. I couldn't hear but my grandaddy snorin' and the birds, the noises they made in the wood. I wouldn't be surprised if I heard a wolf too. There was a terrible lot of noise in that old dark wood.

"George," I said. It was a good name right enough, but it wasn't sich a good name as Rover. I put my head under the blankets and went to sleep.

3

Next day my gramma and my grandaddy thought Harry was at school, but Harry was not at school. Harry was down at the hut with the babby and me. Harry was very sleepy on account of he had been too cold to sleep hardly all night, and so he lay in the hut alongside the babby's nest and slept, and I had the babby to myself. I and the babby had a fine time. The babby had three teeth and a brown spot that wouldn't wash off under its chin. It could stand holdin' on, but it didn't aim to stand on its own. I reckon it was a real lazy kind of babby. It was hard to please with its rations too. It did not like salted ham, and it even did not like a tasty hunk of cheese. It liked water and root, and it wanted to eat a stick of wood, but I did not let it until I had washed the stick good in the lake, and then I told the babby it was jest to sook.

When Harry waked up he sent me to the house for sweet taters, and I got that. Then he sent me to the house for a chunk off my gramma's bolt of cotton, that was for wettin' cloths for the babby, he said to wait till my gramma was out the back, then git the big shears and cut off a hunk this size, he showed me, but I could not work the shears. I got the beginnin' of a hole made, then my hand stuck in the handle of the shears and the blade of the shears stuck in the cloth and I thought I heard my gramma comin', and I picked up the whole bolt and shears an' all and ran; it was bigger'n me that cloth, and it tripped my legs, and I could not see where I was goin', and it got real dirty and scratched with us fallin' and I lost the shears some place and could not find them, but Harry said never mind, my gramma did not see me, nobody did, that was all that signified.

I had to go up to the house for my dinner, and I got some in my pockets for Harry and up my jersey too; my grandaddy was not there, and I did not have to say long prayers, and when I got back Harry had a fire built and the sweet taters was roastin' on the fire. We had ample rations, but the babby was plumb finnicky and would not eat its tater, only a mite when it got cold, and a half slice of bread.

Harry watched the sun. He knew the size of the trees' shadders on the lake, and when they was the right size he said it was time for him to be outa school, and he better had go work a hand on that little old goat afore my gramma, she got there.

"Same as yestiddy, Dave," he said. "It's all yourn till I get back." He meant the babby.

I went and looked to see had he really gone, and then I came back and pulled the babby outa its nest, the babby was hollerin', and set it on my knee.

"Wheesht now, you're my babby now," I said, "Rover."

When Harry came back he was shakin' his head. Wasn't no milk but a little, it was a spoon's fill in the bottom of the tin. "Go up to the house, Dave," Harry said, "and git some pure water for mixin' in." The babby was smart. When it saw the tin it started declarin'. "Hurry, Dave," Harry said, so I went runnin'.

I near run right into my grandaddy.

My grandaddy was standin' in the clearing and a big man along of him. That man was Mister McIver the preacher, and he was the dominie too. He was a true Christian like my grandaddy, he was fierce as a wolf, and his beard was red.

"You! Go git Harry," my grandaddy said, and his voice was small but bad.

I turned and ran back into the trees. I ran my fastest to the hut.

"Red Kiver, Harry!" I said. "Red Kiver, the dominie! And my grandaddy wants you."

"Where?" Harry said. "Where, where, Dave?"

"In the clearing." I pointed.

Harry laid the babby in its nest and turned his eyes to Heaven.

"My grandaddy's hoppin' mad," I said, "on account of he must of got ketched with his boots not on. You better hurry."

"Lord sweet God, have mercy on me," Harry said. "A poor sinner."

I took his hand and we went up to the clearing.

"Come here," my grandaddy said. He pointed Harry with his beard. "Here." And Harry went and stood at the end of his beard. "Now," my grandaddy said, "you stand for judgment. Hev you aught to say?"

Harry shook his head, he did not look.

"The boy has sinned doubly. He has been absent two days," the dominie said, and he limbered his arm. "I maun thrash him, Jim."

"Ay," my grandaddy said, "you maun thrash him, John. This is fair an' fitten since you are his dominie, but you will thrash him in the school's time, I say, an' not in mine."

A glare got up between my grandaddy and the dominie, their eyes stuck out like the prongs of forks.

"I came as friend, Jim."

"You kin go as friend, John," my grandaddy said, "if you so please. You spoke as dominie. A man sends his childer to school, the dominie has the use of that childer in school-time. But when the school is out, a man has the use of his own childer and his childer's childer, and on my land an' in my time no man thrashes mine but me. Harry, git to the woodshed. An' you, Davy, go up to the house for your rations."

I went to the house.

"I never called you yit," my gramma said. "What ails you?"

"Nothing," I said. I sat on my stool at the corner of the fire and wisht for a miracle to deliver Harry from the Christians.

After a long time my grandaddy came stompin' in, I couldn't look.

"What was John McIver the preacher after?" my gramma said.

"It was John McIver the dominie," my grandaddy said. "He came by with a search party. They is searchin' the upper wood an' he stopped by to query for Harry. Harry has been absent the school two days syne."

My gramma opened her mouth and took that in. "And where is Harry?" she asked.

"In the woodshed."

"Hev you beat him?" my gramma said. Her face was shut up tight, and sour.

"No," my grandaddy said. "That is for the dominie. I have ast Harry where he has been and what he has been doin', but he does not aim to tell me. He defies me, an' so I hev shut him in the woodshed, an' he will bide there until he sees the error of his ways. He will git no rations but water. We will now pray."

After we had et, my gramma gave me a cat's lick at the water-shelf and sent me to my bed. I thought mebbe my grandaddy would go and git Harry, and my grandaddy did go to the woodshed, but he came back single. My gramma spoke for Harry, but my grandaddy hit the table a smack and said, "Silence! I have said he bides, woman. An' bide he will."

It was dark.

I put on my clothes and opened the windy enough to git through. There was more noises than any other night, and the ground was a long way down from the windy and I could not see it. I did not want to go, but I knew somebody had to guard the babby from the wild beasts and give it its feed. I put my legs over and hung by my hands. I hung for a long time. After a bit I thought I would climb in again, but I couldn't. I couldn't let go neither. If my grandaddy hadn't been there I'd have hollered for my gramma. I jest hung by my fingers till they bent up. Then I fell. I wasn't hurt except my fingers was sore and my knees was scraped.

It was awful dark.

If somebody got lost on a dark night like that they'd mebbe never git found for days, and if they went down by the hemlocks they might fall into the lake too. The beasts was prowlin' around the wood, you could hear them, and the birds was screamin' with fright.

I went to the woodshed and shouted, "Harry."

I gave a whole heap of kicks on the door and shouted, "Harry, Harry, Harry."

"Is that you, Dave?" Harry said.

"It's me," I said. "Harry, I'm not feart. Harry, mebbe I can't find the hut down by the hemlocks an'll fall into the lake. But I'm not feart, not of the wolves neither."

"I can't hear you," Harry said. "Dave, when you git down there, give the babby its drink and change its wettin' cloth. Can you do that, Dave?"

I didn't know could I or not. I was watchin' a square-shaped beast the size of an ox, it was hidden in back of a bush.

"And then," Harry said, "see the babby is warm and tucked low in its nest, and you can top it up with my gramma's cloth too."

"Harry," I said, "and I can't get back in the windy, it's too high. Harry, there's a great big beast out here glowerin' at me."

"There's what?"

"A great big beast," I said. "But I'm not feart."

"Stop screamin'," Harry said. "It don't do any good to scream."

"I'm not screamin'," I said. "I'm not feart, Harry, even if there's two of them. Harry, will it soon be light?"

"No, it won't be light for a long time," Harry said. "Dave, is there truly a beast? Are you awful feart?"

I could hear my heart, and my hair was hot.

"Are you, Dave?"

"Yes," I said. "And I'm feart of the wolves too, and mebbe I'll fall in the lake and I can't git back in the windy and could be I got lost in the wood and never was found again."

"Well, shet up for a minute," Harry said, "and let me think."

I shet up. I never looked near the beast again, but it took a step nearer and breathed on the back of my neck.

"Harry," I said, "are you still there, thinkin'?"

"Yes," Harry said. "Listen, Dave, there is only one thing for it. You are too little to do for the babby. Go on up to the house and tell my gramma. Tell her about the babby needs its milk. Go on now, run."

I couldn't run. I couldn't move.

"Go on," Harry said. "Dave, hev you gone?"

I heard the beast again and I let out a great loud scream. I guess mebbe I thought I would scare that beast away. I jest stood with my eyes shut and the scream kept skirlin' outa me.

"Dave, is that you, Dave? Where are you?" my grandaddy's voice said, and I opened my eyes and saw his lantern.

"Tell my grandaddy!" Harry said. He was shoutin' and hammerin' on the inside of the shed. "That's grandaddy. Tell grandaddy!"

I ran like a tiger and took a leap at my grandaddy's legs.

"It's the babby," I said. "The babby, Grandaddy!"

He picked me up level with his face and I told him. His face was lamp-lit and queer.

"In the hut by the hemlocks," I said.

"Show me," he said.

I took him down by the hemlocks. The beasts was fair feart of my grandaddy and was all runnin' far away. We heard the babby's holler, and my grandaddy put his face to the sound and widened his legs, and I had to run to keep with him.

The babby was crinkled up and red with its holler, but it let off when it saw the lantern. It was okay. I had to laugh, I was that pleased. "It's mine and Harry's, Grandaddy," I told him. "Our babby."

My grandaddy dug his hand under the babby and lifted it, nest an' all, like in a shovel.

"And that's its milk," I said. "In the tin."

My grandaddy went out the door of the hut and up through the hemlocks towards the house. I was behind and I could not see. I kept fallin'. I ran fast as a hoss, but there was little trees I could not see, and I was scratched an' bleedin' and times I fell in the marsh, and I could not ketch my grandaddy.

"Grandaddy, what are you goin' to do with it?" I cried.

He never said nothing.

"Wait for me, Grandaddy," I said.

But he never waited, no nor spoke.

I got feart all of a sudden. I was very, very feart. "It's mine and Harry's," I shouted. "It's ourn!"

In the clearing I fell too, but I could run faster then and I ketched him up. I clawed at his leg, but his leg was movin' and I fell.

"It's ourn," I said. "Ourn."

My grandaddy pushed open the door and went in the house, and I fell on the step and was too tired and sad to git up. I jest lay screamin'. "Don't eat it, Grandaddy," I said. "Tain't fitten. Please, please don't eat it."

My gramma ran and picked me up and rocked me in her

arms like I was a babby myself. "There ain't nobody goin' to eat it," she said, "or harm a hair of its mite head. Your grandaddy's going to give it back to its rightful owners, and that is all."

"But it's ourn," I cried. "It's mine and Harry's!"

"Hush now," my gramma said, "it's the Donaldson babby, must be. It's been lost two days, an' all the folks from the Houses searchin' for it, an' its mamma an' daddy near demented."

My grandaddy took the babby to the Houses, and that same night the men came for Harry. They came on hosses. They was hard-faced men, and they stood in a crowd inside the door.

"It's the law," they said.

My gramma kissed Harry and buttoned his coat.

"You'll take good care o' him?" she asked.

"He won't come to no harm along of us, ma'am," they said. "The mob won't git him."

And then they set him on a hoss and took him away, and the next day but one they tried him.

4

The store was the court. There was a big space in the middle of the store, and it was all filled up with folks settin' on benches, there must a been twenty there, and my grandaddy and me sat on the front bench. It was Mister Cameron's store, so it was Mister Cameron's court, Tom Cameron, and he sat on a high chair behind the counter, and a writer next to him. The writer was from up the river.

Harry had a chair to hisself.

A skinny man in black cloth got up on his feet. He was hairless and a stranger, and he began the gab.

"The case for the Crown," he said. "Duction of young female." Sometimes he pointed at Harry. He spoke for a long time and folks humphed on their seats and scraped their boots; he spoke quiet and used long words; he was not worth listenin' to. "The Crown rests," he said, and sat down.

"Accused," Tom Cameron said.

Sam Howie, standin' back of Harry, poked him with his finger and Harry stood up.

"Harry Mackenzie, you got anythin' to say?" Tom Cameron said.

"The Lord have mercy on me," Harry said. "I am eight years old and a sinner, but I aimed at no harm."

"You understand," Tom Cameron said, "this is your defence. Is that all you got to say?"

"Yes, mister," Harry said.

"Sir," the writer said. "You call the court sir."

"Yes, mister," Harry said.

Sam Howie poked him with his finger again and Harry sat down. That was the best thing of all. That was right smart. Every time Sam Howie poked Harry he stood up, and if he was standing he sat down. I grinned to Harry, but he was feart to smile back on account of my grandaddy. My grandaddy was settin' with his arms folded and his beard up. He never moved a half-inch.

"Well, then," Tom Cameron said, "this is how it looks to me. First, this female child has not come to a deal of harm. That's right, Bill, isn't it? Where's Bill Donaldson?"

"I'm here," Bill Donaldson said, and he stood up. He was the babby's daddy. "Ain't harmed none far as me and my missus can see. Got to admit that."

"Well, then," Tom Cameron said, "on the other side nobody can't deny there's been too much of this particler kind of lawlessness hereabouts. Take last month only. Willie Fleming's daughter. It was that trapper from your way, it was up the river, what was his name, Arch?"

"Foster," the writer said.

"That Foster," Tom Cameron said. "We all know what he did. He had Willie's Sarah off in the woods for twelve days afore the law caught up on him. Well, then we made him marry her right here in this court, and Sarah's got a man and tied up regler and Willie's well pleased, admitted; still an' all, this abductions and crimes has got to cease."

"Sex crimes," the writer said.

"That's right," Tom Cameron said. "Sex crimes too. Our women rate high with us in this community and, rightly, a woman's purity is a hangin' matter. It was time we showed the wild elements that this is so, and a man tampers with womenfolk gits his just deserts."

There was a kind of soft growl from most everybody, and Tom Cameron nodded right and left and pointed to Harry. "Well, then," he said, "we got here a boy who is guilty of the kidnap and abduction of this young female Margaret, daughter of Bill Donaldson. He says he aimed at no harm, and according to Bill he did no harm, but he admits to kidnap, and that is a hangin' crime and has caused a deal of worry to Bill Donaldson and his missus."

"Darn right," Bill Donaldson said.

"Well, now," Tom Cameron said, "we do not aim to be hangin' an eight-year-old boy, and the clerk says they will not take him upriver in the prison, but I hear there is schools for young uns where they can be teched to be reformed, and it is my opinion that we should conseeder the sendin' of Harry Mackenzie to one of them reform schools. Does happen anyone in the court knows aught of them schools?"

My grandaddy stood up and looked round the court, face to face. Nobody spoke, and then my grandaddy looked at Tom Cameron. "If you send him to a school, Tom," my grandaddy said, "I'll shoot you."

"Sit down, Jim," Tom Cameron said, "and don't interfere with the course of justice."

"Contempt of court," the writer said.

"You shet up," my grandaddy said, "you scribblin' Pharisee. As for you, Tom, you know me well, an' you hev my meaning." And he sat down.

"Well, now," Tom Cameron said, and he clucked in his throat and blinked like a little fat owl. "We was saying. I take it nobody here knows aught of them schools?"

"I could find out," the writer said.

"So you could," Tom said. "So you could. You will notice, Jim, that I did not say we was goin' to send the boy to a reform school. All I said was, did anybody know aught of them schools so as the court could conseeder them. Well, now, it seems to me that the cause of justice would be served if the Clerk here was to find out all about them reform schools and then the court will have the information it needs and can send Harry Mackenzie to a reform school if it thinks fit the *next time* he appears on a similar charge. Case dismissed. That's all to-day, folks."

Sam Howie poked Harry with his finger and Harry stood up. "You're let aff," Sam said.

Everybody got up, started movin' and speakin'. "Store's now open," Tom Cameron said, shoutin'. "Anybody aims to buy."

"Harry," my grandaddy said, "come here."

Harry came.

"Hullo, Harry," I said.

He never spoke or looked at me. He was white as sickly and his eyes was set low.

"Take Davy home," my grandaddy said. "Git straight home, the both of you, and you Harry set on your chair and wait there till I get home. Do you hear me?"

"Yis," Harry said. He whispered.

"Git movin' then," my grandaddy said.

Harry took my hand and we went home.

"You feelin' okay, Harry?" I asked.

"Yis," Harry said. "But there is an awful thing happened. Dave, you guess what's happened? My grandaddy got his boots on, and you know what is in the inside of them boots. It was the left boot."

I stared at him. I had clean forgot.

"The picture," Harry said. "The picture of the dawgs."

"Ah God," I said.

"So I will git two thrashings," Harry said. "Thrashed on account of the babby and thrashed on account of the picture."

"Mebbe I will git thrashed too," I said.

We went straight but slow.

"If he beats me till the blood comes," Harry said, "I am goin' to run away. Happen there is bits of my behind that I cannot see myself, so you will look for me, Dave, and if there is blood shows I will run away."

"I will run away too, Harry," I said.

"I am not goin' to stay and be beat to death," Harry said. "If he bloods me I will truly run away."

"Me too," I said.

I thought about runnin' away. I wondered where we would run to.

"Harry," I said. "That babby. It was a girl babby."

"Yis," Harry said. "Kin you walk faster, Dave?"

"Me? Easy," I said.

"Well," Harry said, "we better."

We walked fast. I thought of the places I knew. We could not run away to the Houses on account of we would only git ketched, and we could not run away to the woods on account of there was only beasts in the wood and there would be nobody to give us our meat.

"My gramma is makin' a pie," I said.

"What kind?" Harry asked.

"I forgit."

"Was it a berry pie?"

"I purely forgit," I said. "Harry, mebbe my gramma would run away with us too. That would be fine, wouldn't it, Harry?"

"No," Harry said. "She is on his side."

"My grandaddy spoke up for you in the court," I said. "He was on our side then, Harry."

"Yis, of course," Harry said. "But that is with strangers. Him an' her is on the same side in the family. You tell my gramma a word of this about runnin' away and I will not take you with me. I mean that, Dave."

"All right," I said. But I felt sad. "I won't tell. I swear it, Harry."

We got to the house and went in.

"So you're home," my gramma said. "And hongry, I'll be bound."

"No, I ain't hongry," Harry said.

"Ain't hongry!" my gramma said. "I never. Well, I know somebody that is."

"Me neither," I said.

"I got a pie. Blackberry pie."

"I ain't hongry, Gramma," Harry said.

He sat down on his chair at the corner of the fire and I sat on my stool. My gramma stood starin'.

"We're waitin' for my grandaddy," I said. "My grandaddy said set and wait for him."

"Oh," my gramma said. She wiped her hands on her apron and shut her mouth up tight, and after a minute she turned to the skillet.

We waited a long time.

My gramma put the knives and tools on the table. "Even though you ain't hongry," she said, "you jest had better eat."

"Listen, there's my grandaddy!" Harry said.

I listened.

"Hear him?" Harry said. Harry was begun to shake, and me too, my knees was jiggin'.

My grandaddy opened the door and my gramma slammed the pie on the table. She stood and stared, jest stared.

"You sold them, then, you really did it!" she said. I looked where she was lookin', and saw that my grandaddy was bare-fit. "You walked through the Houses in your bare feet, Jim!"

"They are clean," my grandaddy said. "My good name is in God's hands and my pride does not rest in ornaments. Harry, git your gramma the quill and parchment."

Harry's hands was not trusty. He dropped the quill on the floor and I ran and picked it up.

"He will write it his own self," my gramma said. She spoke firm. "Harry will."

My grandaddy did not argue.

"Sit down, Harry," my gramma said.

My grandaddy plucked a paper outa his pocket and laid it on the table. Harry began to cry. I never seen Harry cry in all my life before. I looked at the paper. It was the picture of the dawgs.

"Take up the quill an' write," my grandaddy said. "Write this: 'Sir, I here enclose $26.50 for one red setter dawg and carriage of same stop in good condition and oblige.' Hev you writ that?"

Harry shook his head.

"Well, write it," my grandaddy said.

"And add this," my gramma said. "Yours in good faith." She was smilin' pretty as a young mamma, and she spoke slow and proud. "Yours in good faith," she said. "James Mackenzie."

Harry wrote like fury; my grandaddy leaned over to see every scratch, and my gramma put her hand on my head.

"We're goin' to git a dawg," I said. "Are we, Gramma?"

"Yis," she said, smilin'. "Yis, Davy."

"I reckon we'll call it Rover," I said. "Eh, Harry?"

Harry looked up for a minute and nodded, grinnin', and my grandaddy nodded too. "Rover's a right enough name," he said. I stood close up with my chin on the table, watchin'. I was mighty content, not only on account of the dawg, but on account of I now knew ours was a good family, not like some. In our family we was all on the same side.

CROWNING GLORY

ALTHOUGH I HAVE LIVED MY LIFE AMONG PROFESSIONAL artists of one kind or another, I have known only one complete, one truly great single-minded artist. Her name (for the purpose of this story) was Jane Simmond Lindsay, and—God forgive Himself—she is dead. She was strong and healthy, and I did not ever think that she would die within an imaginable time. I used to hate it when she spoke of death.

"Johnny," she said more than once, "when I die you'll write my biography, won't you?"

"You won't ever die," I said. "The day you die the sun will collide with the moon and the earth will melt. Now shut up, Jane."

"All right," she said. "But you will write my biography, won't you? And, Johnny, call it something simple. Call it the Story of an Artist. Will you do that, Johnny?"

"No," I said. "Even if you died I wouldn't write about you, Jane. I couldn't. And anyway, your life's not a job for a commercial hack like me. I'm just not good enough."

"Johnny," she said, and her voice saying it is in my ear now, "Johnny, you're the only person in all the world who is good enough. You're the only one who knows me."

And that was true, of course. I was the only person who knew Jane Lindsay. I knew her better than I knew anyone, but, despite all that you may have heard, I was not technically her lover. I did not have that degree of knowledge, and neither did any other man. Although she was known as the last of the great professional beauties and credited with the prowess that belongs to such a title, she was, in fact, her own woman, even at thirty-six; and she died that way.

The accident in which Jane was killed took place at 11.03 on the 2nd of November at the Littlehamsley level crossing, and on the 5th—yes, Guy Fawkes' Day—Melanie and I drove down to Esher for the private service at Jane's house. Melanie had on a new hat and, under her mink, a new black costume with a bit of something white and virginal at the throat. She was dressed to bury, and I suppose it would not have occurred to anyone except myself that she was also dressed to kill.

"I can't help it, can I," she said, "if black happens to suit me?"

She sat touching, demurely feline, with a knee exposed and available against the gear lever close to my hand. She was properly quiet and subdued, outwardly unexceptionable; but inside he was purring. I knew, yet did not hate her for it. She was my wife.

"I hope," she said, "I do hope everything goes off all right, Johnny."

"This is not a dress rehearsal or a first night," I said. "There is nothing to go wrong."

"There'll be such a crowd," Melanie said. "And you know what Jane was. How everybody loved her. What I was thinking of was just this, that somebody might break down, that was all. Will I light you another cigarette?"

"If that is an oblique reference to me, Melanie," I said, "you can stop worrying. I'm not the breaking-down kind. I won't disgrace you."

"I'm sure you won't, darling," Melanie said. "Do you think you should drive so fast? We don't want to be the first to arrive, do we?"

"I suppose not," I said. "We might even seem to be gloating. It wouldn't look too well, would it?"

"No, darling, I don't think it would."

I eased down, and we had the strain in silence for a bit, which was how I liked it best. Then Melanie sank down into her shoulders and put her knee on the dashboard and said, "Johnny, please, please remember this one thing, whatever else. I love you. I'm not jealous any more. There's nothing left to be jealous of any more. I just love you. Johnny, please!"

"I'll take that cigarette, thanks," I said. "Did I tell you Sam Schultz rang this morning? He said they want me to extend the Zanzibar serial fifteen thousand words. He said to remember him to you. He wanted to know what would happen to the show now. He thought it would close down, but I said no, Becky wouldn't let this beat him, he'd get somebody to take her place."

"Nobody ever could take Jane's place, ever," Melanie said.

"That's what Sam said too."

"Nobody could ever take her place with you either, could she, Johnny?"

"I guess not," I said.

I was slow to see that she was crying. It was such a discreet performance that, until the handkerchief came out, I could not know if I was meant to notice.

"You've your best face," I said.

"Oh, go to hell!" Melanie said, releasing a vulgar slobber of sound, as if it were an ordinary human being crying and not an actress at all. I put my arm along the back of the seat and she turned her face to me and cried on my sleeve.

"Don't hate me. Please stop hating me, Johnny," she said.

I could not think of anything to say, and I put my hand under her arm and lifted her off breast in a manner that I hoped was affectionate. I did this several times, and she stopped crying and regularised her breathing.

"I *am* sorry Jane's dead. I am truly," she said. "You do believe that, don't you, Johnny?"

"Yes," I said.

I had to change down, and as we were now in a traffic line on the outskirts of the town, I did not replace my arm. Melanie took out her gadgets and remade her face like new. It was a good face, and easy to work on. I smiled to it and it smiled back to me, and we turned decorously up the drive to Jane's place, a man and wife like any other, presenting, I think, a front good enough to fool anyone who did not already know.

2

Mrs. Burnett, Jane's dresser, had taken charge. Although I had always treated her as a person in her own right, I had done so merely for policy, and I was faintly surprised at her hand-grip and her sure eyes.

"I'll take you upstairs, Mrs. Sadler," she said. "Mr. Sadler, you'll find everybody in the lounge. And Mr. Campbell, of Campbell & Stein, is here and wants to see you. He's in the library with the papers."

I put my hat and coat in the closet behind the door. Some of Jane's heavy coats were still on the hangers, and their faint perfume struck home immediately and accompanied me across the hall to the library, where Whitney Campbell, Jane's lawyer, abruptly laid down a cardboard box and advanced, hand first, to greet me. "Ha, John!" he said, being hearty, laying a plane for us to meet on. "Wondered when you would get here. You look fine. A bit peaked perhaps, but fine. Yes, fine." He probed me with his tactless, energetic eyes. "Melanie with you?"

"Of course," I said. "And I feel fine, thank you. Let's cut the usual cackle, Whit, and get down to the business in hand. I understand that you and I are joint executors. Is that correct?"

"Perfectly."

"Is there any complication, any irregularity?"

"None whatsoever. Poor Jane's affairs have always been, as you know, in my hands, and I think I may truthfully say . . ."

"Of course, of course, Whit," I said. "Well, what's the figure?"

"The estate? Including the insurance, but excluding the two houses, just over a hundred and twenty thousand. Of course, that figure will be whittled down by the death duties, but there will still be a reasonable little sum for the ward, Miss Marshall. You've met her?"

"The niece, you mean? No, I haven't met her."

"She's here now. Charming girl, although without the slightest resemblance to Jane. You know, I suppose, that Jane hasn't left you anything. You know why, don't you?"

"Yes," I said.

"She didn't want to take a step that would give rise to any sort of talk."

"It's all right," I said. "I said I knew why, didn't I?"

"You mustn't let it upset you, John," Whit said. "There always is talk. I mean, a woman like Jane. She was a public figure. You saw that wonderful obituary in *The Times*, didn't you? The last and one of the greatest of the great professional beauties. Such a woman can't have a private, a really private, life. There is always bound to be speculation and gossip in certain quarters, and I must say, as I have said frankly to you before, John, that you tended to lay yourself open to the innuendo. You were not always discreet."

"Please, Whit," I said. "Please." I was getting very tired of Whit. I did not want him to get me talking, because I knew that, once started, I would say more than I wanted to say and far, far more than Whit wanted to hear. He had been in love with Jane, of course, and Jane, as far as I knew, never noticed. She accepted love as other women accept courtesy. You had to make it physical if you wanted Jane to notice.

"However," Whit said, "that's a thing of the past. The public memory is notoriously short. I think it was very sensible of you to bring Melanie. Must be nearly three months since I saw Melanie. And now, if you'd care to glance through these papers, and yes, there's one other item which, frankly, I can hardly bring myself to discuss. A box, with a bill for seventy-five guineas, arrived this morning. From a trichologist, he calls himself."

"This box?" I said, pointing.

"Yes. It came by registered post."

"What's in it, then?"

"Well," Whitney said, "it's a wig."

3

I looked at my watch as I left the library. Two twenty-five. Five minutes to zero hour. I had the zero-hour stomach as I crossed No Man's Land to the lounge. Mrs. Burnett, coming downstairs, said "Hist!" to halt me, closed, and pressed my hand. "I'm sorry, Mr. Sadler," she whispered. "Sorry."

"I'm sorry, too," I said, smiling.

"Ah, God," she said, and, adjusting her face to impassivity, preceded me into the lounge. They were all there, all the people I expected, the tycoons and the sycophants, the people to whom Jane had meant money.

"David," I said. "Hullo. Hullo, Jake. Priscilla."

Melanie was over by the south window. I ignored her urgent eyebrow and cut east through a gaggle of thin, curtly dressed women. "Johnny," they said, hushed. "Johnny"—the more important ones said Mr. Sadler—"hullo."

"Girls," I said, giving them my teeth for spite, the full McLean.

"Poor Johnny," they said, disappointed, watching my back going away.

Philip Kidd, seeing me, wrenched out of a tight group and seized my hand in both of his. "My God, Johnny," he said, "isn't it terrible! I don't know how to face you. I swear I wasn't at fault. My God, Jane of all people. There was nothing I could have done, but I'll never stop blaming myself. I wish to God it had been me. I'll never drive that car again. I'm going to sell it."

"That's all right, all right, Kiddo," I said.

"No, but I mean it, Johnny. I wish to God it had been me. I really wish that, Johnny."

I saw that I was expected to say something. "So do I," I said, and went on, the spotlight following.

Joe Gregory was up by the fireplace in confab with J. C. Flink, the backer, and I mean J. C. Joe was plain Joe, thank God, even at this sort of function. He nodded—no hand flannel—"Ho, Johnny!"

"Hullo, Mr. Sadler," J. C. said, shaking hands. "I'm glad to see you. This is a shocking affair, isn't it? We can ill-afford a loss of this magnitude. It certainly is a sad blow to the English stage and screen."

"Not to mention the box-office," I said.

"What's that? True, true." He gave me the famous rapid blink—the Flink blink. He wasn't sure of me. He doubted if I was quite reliable, and he was such a big man that it was good business to let the doubt sit on his face. He had been considering me for a long time, measuring me for a niche in the Flink organisation, another tame writer to be kept in the box next to Joe's, but he couldn't make up his mind. Damn his eyes, I'd have taken the lousy job too, and he knew it. I needed that kind of money. "A terrible tragedy," he said. "Truly terrible. Do you happen to have the time?"

"Twenty-eight minutes past," I said. "You're looking well, Mr. Flink."

"I feel fine. Feel all right, you know. But I have to be careful. It's my chest. I had pneumonia a year ago, you may remember. Of course, I'm all right now, but it's this weather, damp, Joseph was just saying; well, I mean, we're none of us getting any younger and at my age you've got to be careful, you know. I say, Joseph, it *is* Adelie Roberts. Fancy Adelie coming all the way down from Town. . . ." His voice drifted off in Adelie's direction and his trim person followed.

"Well, Johnny," Joe said, "you just keep it up; you keep up that nice line of small talk, and you'll get your diamond collar all right, yes sir, the grade A Flink collar for grade A Flink flunkeys. Did you see the size of my credit in *The Lady in the Chair*? I got that just by dishing up a few sirs the week they edited. 'Yes, Mr. Flink,' I said. 'Yes, sir.' Just the way I said it to you back there. I reckon it didn't cost me more than a cubic centimetre of soul. You ought to get wise, chum. Get commercial with a capital C. No, don't say it, Johnny. Please don't say it in here. Melanie's looking well."

"Melanie's a fine-looking girl," I said. "Even without her face on she's a fine-looking girl. Melanie always looks well, Joe. I say, Joe, I can't help feeling it. They're talking, aren't they?"

"Jane?" Joe said. "I'm afraid so. It was that fat bum, the lawyer. He only mentioned it to one or two of us, in strictest confidence. You know the line. Nobody to breathe a word. Now, naturally, it's the only topic. You knew all along, I suppose?"

I nodded. I was on a beam with Melanie, and I was fighting not to hate her for the naked triumph in her eyes.

"It's shaken everybody back on their heels," Joe said. "By God, when you think of it, she was a remarkable woman, Johnny, she really was, you know."

"She was a great artist," I said.

"Listen, Joe," I said, and it was suddenly so important that I had him by the lapels, "she was a truly great artist. Besides being the finest woman I ever met, she was the greatest artist of our time. You know what she's asked for on the stone? Just the plain words: 'She Was An Artist.' She was proud of that, and she had reason to be. She was superlatively an artist. She was, Joe."

"I believe you, Johnny," Joe said. "As you know, I didn't know her very well, but I certainly appreciated her work. I often went to see her twice and even three times in a part, and I certainly thought she was lovely. God, it makes you want to cry. See that old boy over by the window? They tell me he's from the hospital, but it's kind of embarrassing, nobody knows whether he's a professor or whether he's just here to take the body away. What did she want to go and do a thing like that for, anyway, sell her body to a hospital? She was always so damned fastidious about crossing her legs and all that kind of thing. What could have got into her, would you know, Johnny?"

"She was hard up," I said. "It was a long time, nearly twenty years ago, when she lost her first job in repertory. Do you know what she got? She got three pounds, Joe."

"But why didn't she buy it back? You can buy back your body like any other transaction on the pop, can't you?"

"I don't know," I said. "When Jane made a bargain she stuck to it. Maybe that was it. She told me she was mighty grateful for that three pounds at the time. Hullo, Mrs. Burnett."

"Mr. Sadler," Mrs Burnett said, breathing on me, "I didn't think to ask you. Do you want to go upstairs?"

"Upstairs?"

"To see her."

"No," I said. "No, thank you, Mrs. Burnett. I'd rather not."

"I thought if you wanted to go you'd just go on up by yourself," Mrs. Burnett said. "I thought when you didn't go it must be because you didn't want to go, but then I thought too I might just as well make sure. And I thought you would like to know that there's no reason at all why you shouldn't go up and see her. She looks very peaceful, you would really never know it was an accident."

"Thank you very much, Mrs. Burnett," I said. "But I won't go."

"I see everybody is looking at the time," Mrs. Burnett said. "I hope they won't think this is my fault. I rang up five minutes ago to make sure he'd left, and they said the Canon had been detained, he was just leaving, and I'm sure I don't know how long it'll take him to get here on these greasy roads. Have you seen Mrs. Black, Mr. Sadler? I'm sure she would be heartened to have a kindly word from you."

"Poor Blackie!" I said. "Mrs. Black is the housekeeper." I said to Joe, "So she hasn't got another job yet, has she?"

"Well, that's a part of the trouble," Mrs. Burnett said. "She's had offers, of course, but they haven't come up to her expectations. And when you put it like that, I must say she hasn't been a lot of help to me all through this unhappy time. I think I'd better go and explain to everybody what the delay is. Theatrical people are so difficult, I always think, when there's a crowd of them gets together."

"A nice woman," Joe said. "A nice fat woman. It is a pleasure to see a woman who is nice and fat and uncomplicated for a change."

I watched her going away. Of all the people in this room she was probably the only person, apart from myself, who had really known Jane and loved her. The others had known only the myth. They had respected Jane and they had liked to be known as her friends. Perhaps even they had genuinely liked her, but the warmth of their affection had been tempered by the awe that Jane's beauty and Jane's technique always engendered. They had been hem-of-the-garment friends. Only Burnett and I had ever got through to the skin. Only Burnett and I had known the secret that was now so deliciously the life and soul of the party. I looked around at the tight, bright, ravenous faces, at the accurate, deadly mouths and the titillated ears and the eyes that slanted so quickly past me. I listened deliberately to the discreet, upsurging ripple of their modulated voices, and I thought, with sudden loss of control, my God how they stink, I've got to, got to get out of here.

"Joe," I said, "what about a drink?"

"It'll have to be a small one," Joe said. "I've a noggin in the car."

They made way immediately. Even when they had their backs to us they made way immediately. They were that kind of people—extra sensitive—and they had a developed awareness for situations of this sort.

"My God, what a crowd!" I said, out in the hall.

"Our friends," Joe said. "When we finish my noggin we'll get a bottle off of Mrs. Burnett. We'll skip this whole matinée and have a party, what do you say? I don't see why we shouldn't have a good time like everybody else."

"Johnny!" Melanie called, coming out of the lounge in a peremptory swirl of skirts. "Hullo, Joe. Johnny, I want to speak to you."

"Hullo, Melanie," Joe said. "Are you having a lovely bitchy time?"

"Joe, you oughtn't to speak to me like that," Melanie said. "Johnny, you ought not to let him speak to me like that. My God, this is no picnic for me, do you think? Johnny, please, I want to speak to you."

"What is it?"

"I want to speak to you privately. Upstairs. Just for a minute, Johnny."

"Wait for me. I won't be long, Joe," I said.

I followed Melanie upstairs to the first landing.

"Listen, Johnny, this is important," she said. "In here."

"Hell, Melanie," I said. "This is a bathroom."

"It's private," Melanie said, and she locked the door. "Now look, Johnny, there's something you've got to know. I don't suppose you've heard, because nobody would tell it to you, although everybody is talking about it, but it's something you've got to know, and it's best you should hear it from me. It's about Jane, Johnny. She wore a wig. She hadn't a hair of her own on her head. Yes, I know it's incredible, but it's true. Her head was bare, stark naked. She was bald as a billiard ball."

I leaned against the bathroom wall and looked away from Melanie because she was my wife, a lovely girl, and I did not want to see the ugly thing in her eyes. I wondered who had told her that Jane's head was bald as a billiard ball. It was not the sort of simile that would have struck her in a hundred years.

"Who told you that?" I said.

"I don't know. Everybody's talking about it. It's absolutely true."

"About the billiard ball, I mean. I didn't know you were *au fait* with billiard balls."

"For God's sake, Johnny," Melanie said, "didn't you hear what I said? Jane was bald. Bald, Johnny. I'm not just making it up. It's true. She was bald worse than a man, and it was a wig she wore."

I uncrossed my legs, stood up off the wall, and put a cigarette in my mouth. "I know," I said. I was trembling a little, but only in the legs.

"You're lying," Melanie said. "You couldn't have known. I mean, you couldn't. She not only had it fixed with clips, but with a kind of glue too. She spent a fabulous fortune on it. Nobody could have known, and least of all you. It just wouldn't make sense if you knew."

"Nevertheless," I said, "I knew."

She put a hand on her throat and stared. "But you couldn't, just couldn't have!"

"Melanie," I said, "Jane was an artist. Can I ever get you to understand it? You're shocked, disgusted because she wore a wig, and you seem to think that *I* should be too. Can't you understand that it was this above all other things which emphasised Jane's genius? It was this I—admired her most for. Jane was a great artist, the sort of person you meet only once in a lifetime. Listen, maybe this will bring it home to you.

There's a wig downstairs now—she had two—which has just been returned by her hairdresser with a bill for seventy-five guineas. Do you know what that seventy-five guineas was for? It was for the addition of eleven grey hairs. That was the sort of artist Jane was."

"Oh, my God, eleven grey hairs!" Melanie said. "My God!" and she leaned, legs pliant, against the wall and laughed her high round laugh that bounced out of her mouth like a string of golf balls. "Don't hit me," she said.

I turned away quickly, unlocked the door, and went out. Joe was sitting on the bottom step watching for me. "Let's make it snappy," he said, getting up. "I just heard the Bish's car, and I reckon the only way to dodge him is to slip out the back way. Come on, Johnny, get weaving."

"I don't think I'll go, Joe," I said. "It really isn't fair on Melanie. I don't think I ought to."

Melanie came downstairs and laid a hand on my shoulder. She ignored Joe completely. "Johnny," she said, "I just thought of something. I don't suppose it would have occurred to you that in your humble way you too are an artist. A great artist. Yes, you are, Johnny. One hell of a great artist, with my heart."

"You dear, dear things," Joe said. "Now for God's sake let's all go and have that drink. Johnny, you look fit to pass out. Melanie, you can come too and make lots more pretty speeches."

"No, no," Melanie said. "Johnny did not come here for drinks. Nor for pretty speeches even. Johnny came to bury Cæsar, didn't you, darling? Fellow artist, lend me your arm."

"Steady," I said. "Steady, Melanie." But I gave her my arm and, Joe following, we walked slowly back to the lounge.

THE BLACK DEVIL, MAINLY

WHEN I WAS TWELVE YEARS OLD I WITNESSED A REVOLUTION at close range. It was a one-man revolution. The man was my Tio Federico, Uncle Federico, and this revolution took place inside him.

Sometimes an individual would require to know my uncle's occupation, and my uncle would say then that he was a pigeon-fancier, the trainer and possessor of the fastest birds in the world. My aunt used to say other things of him. She used to say he was *simpatico*, a Juan Bragas, a fine, lazy fool of a man.

At this stage it was obligatory for me to intervene.

"But he is passionate," I would remind her.

"That must be conceded," my aunt would say, bringing her thin lips together and nodding in emphasis. "Your uncle is a very passionate man." She used to say this often, and when my uncle had committed one of his excesses, she used to say it in justification. Even when I was a very small girl I knew that it pleased my Tia Maria that my Tio Federico was a passionate man. I knew it was highly creditable, and when I was big enough to go to school I boasted of it. I held up my hand in class, and when I had got the nod I made an announcement of it.

"My uncle is a very passionate man," I said.

The teacher blushed. It interested us to see her blush, because she had a fairer complexion than anyone in the district; she was not a native Andalusian, and thus, being of another species, almost albino like an American film dame, her blush was of a deeper hue. After school she held me in detention.

"You must never say that again," she said, "about your uncle. It is not proper."

"Nevertheless, he is a very passionate man."

"Even so," the teacher said, "one does not speak of it." She had hair the colour of dried vine stalks, a comfortable appearance and a kindly manner. She never corrected us dramatically, and we were all sorry when her time came and she had to leave the school in disgrace.

My uncle's main passions were: (1) his pigeons, (2) his bed, (3) his music, (4) his wine, (5) his women. I am not sure that this is strictly the order of his preference, but it is the order that reflects most credit on him and it is primarily accurate. The pigeons came first.

My uncle's pigeons were celebrated. People used to travel from Cordoba and even from Seville to discuss pigeons with my uncle, and once a char-à-banc containing twenty-six persons stopped at the foot of the hill where the road ends and the persons, all carrying loaves and wineskins like pilgrims, trampled over the young vines and climbed up the hill to our home. They were *aficionados*, experts, from Granada, and included a foreigner who was reputed to have come all the way from England, if you would credit it!

My uncle was always glad to see visitors. "The pigeon wears no uniform and knows no boundaries," he would say. "Welcome to my domain, *amigo*." He would talk to a visitor all day long, sitting in the sun against one of the pigeon-loft stanchions, his legs crossed, his guitar-like *bandurria* across his knees, and his sombrero tilted down over his face so that, standing, you could see only the ends of his long black moustachios waggling without cessation as he talked. My aunt did not object. "In such a man the jaw is the least mischievous of his limbs," she would say. "Let him work it." It was my uncle's duty to stamp the vines in autumn, and for this purpose I washed and polished his feet each Friday, but if a stranger came, my uncle would not consent to stamp the vines. "Let there be due priority," he said. "The time for a man to work is when the relish has gone from his bones." He loved company. If the visitors came before the midday meal he would even get out of his bed to show them the Black Devil and to talk pigeons.

The Black Devil was the best, the most valuable, the most treasured of all my uncle's birds. He was the Champion of Andalusia, and he had averaged 1,870 *metros* per minute in a race of 300 *kilometros*. It was conceded everywhere that he was excessively handsome. He had a large broad head, with intelligent eyes, his back was dark grey, his chest light purple, and there were many colours, including yellow, green and gold, on the sides of his neck. He had a long tail, and the flying feathers in his wings were extremely broad. In a tin box under the bed my uncle kept a letter from a *caballero* in Seville who wished to buy the Black Devil and offered to pay 250 *douros*. It was there in writing, in ink, and I read it myself after I learned how. My uncle used often to make me read it to him. No one at all, not even my aunt, could deny that the Black Devil was a noble bird.

My uncle used to play the *bandurria* and sing *coplas* to him by the hour. In this way, my uncle said, the Black Devil grew very wise, because there was not only art in these songs, there was also all the wisdom of the ages. People laughed at my uncle for playing music to pigeons.

"Fools!" my uncle said. "Do they think I would play to mere pigeons! I play to the Champion only, and to his grandson, the Young Devil, the future Champion of the World."

"But the other birds listen also," I pointed out.

"That is another matter. They can listen if they please. I play only to the Devils."

When people asked my uncle to what he attributed his racing success, he used to hold up his *bandurria*. "I inculcate a musical sense," he would say. "When released from their traps in a race the birds of other breeders return home from habit and for food. My birds return for music. Sweet breath of a virgin, can you wonder that my beauties do not tarry!" And he would begin to strum a gay *seguidilla*, using the index finger of his right hand to pluck the music from the strings. At a market my aunt bought an instrument called a plectrum, which it is traditional to use in conjunction with the *bandurria*, and my uncle used it out of politeness, but after a short time he hid it and said he had lost it. I myself saw him bury it. He preferred to play with his first finger, which was very short and strong and covered with black hairs right down to the nail. He said there was a great deal of tone in this particular finger.

It was when he was a bird of four and I was a girl of eleven that the Black Devil won the Championship of Andalusia. My uncle received a handsome prize. He received 75 *douros*, and that is a great deal of money in any exchange. It was necessary for him to go to Cordoba for the ceremony of award, and he remained away for two weeks. When he returned he had only one *perra gorda*, a penny, which he gave to me, saying he had saved it with great difficulty. He had also, unknown to him, a *peseta* which my aunt found in the lining of his jacket when she was washing this garment.

"*Qué hombre*, what a man!" she said, staring at the coin, and she sat down stiff-backed in the basket-chair with tears running down her cheeks.

"*Mujer!*" my uncle bellowed from the bed. "Woman, how long do you mean to keep me here in punishment?"

"Until your clothes are in a condition fit to wear," my aunt said, jumping up and thrusting her arms into the tub again. "Francesca, go and get your uncle his *bandurria*. This silence is boring holes in me."

"Yes, Auntie," I said.

There were so many stains on my uncle's trousers that they had to be washed several times, and the next day they were still wet. My aunt said he could have permission to wear his other pair provided he sat in careful places, and my uncle took the bottom out of the wicker chair and carried it to his favourite location at the south side of the pigeon-loft, where he could keep an eye on his birds, and at the same time watch everything that happened down in the valley, in particular the *trencorreo*, the train that runs twice each day, once this way and once that, between Seville and Linares.

When I was returning with the goat's milk my uncle called me over.

"Frasquita," he said, "we are going to be very rich. Next year I shall win the Championship of the whole of Spain. Then the year after I shall win the Championship of Europe. Frankly the Belgians do not have a tenth part of my knowledge of birds. The Championship of the Civilised World will fall to me like a wheat-stalk under the sickle, and then we shall have money to throw to the poor. We shall have *paella* to eat every day. We shall have a new loft with electrical appliances, including red and green winking lights that will inform me which birds are out and which birds are in, and we shall have a new house, and you, my little Frasquita, you shall have a room of your own; yes, with a window! And clothes: such clothes as you have never dreamed of—rich brocades, gleaming silks and satins. . . ."

"And a drawer to keep my clothes?" I urged.

"Verily."

"And shoes. Shall I have shoes, *Tio*?"

"Even shoes," my uncle said.

He made the most generous promises of any person in the world. I could have sat all day listening to him if I had not had work to do. When I got up to go away he thought of something else.

"We shall also have employees to tread the vine," he said firmly. "I wish you to note that point, Francesca."

My uncle was a very thirsty man. This was due to his stomach. It was exceedingly large, and it lacked certain of the organs which occupy space in the stomachs of ordinary people. It was therefore impossible to fill. When my uncle explained this to me, he used to drum with his fingers on his stomach so that I could hear how very hollow it was.

"It is the belly of an aristocrat," my uncle would say.

In order to appease his stomach my uncle was prepared to drink almost anything. At home he drank only white wine, because this was all that my aunt permitted. He drank this wine out of a five-litre leather skin, and he could squirt the wine into his mouth in a steady jet at a distance of thirty centimetres. My aunt allowed him to fill his wine-skin only once each day, and he rarely stole any. He did not care for this wine. "The Christian religion is great, truly," he would say. "But this Christian wine is nobody's affair. Baptised wine! Who wishes his wine baptised! Bah! Give me the wine of the Moor, every day!"

When my uncle was away from home he drank *fundador* and *aguardiente* and *anis del mono*. He also drank *manzanilla* and *jerez* and red wine, and he was willing, he said, to drink beer too, if necessary.

When my uncle returned from a *borrachero*, a drinking-bout, he sometimes behaved in a very unusual manner. On one occasion he was a priest, and my aunt and I had to kneel before him with our eyes closed. "Lord," he said, "have mercy on these sinners," and poured a pot of broth over our heads. Fortunately, it was not boiling. On another occasion he was a train—not a *trencorreo*, but a luxury express, first class only, with bed cabins and fearful velocity. Usually, he was the Black Devil. One always knew when he was the Black Devil, because when he was the Black Devil he extended his arms at full length and zoomed all over the room, cooing. On such occasions my aunt sent me under the bed for safety. It was then my duty to impede my uncle with obstacles which I pushed or rolled from underneath the bed, whereupon my aunt would hit my uncle on the head with an unbreakable object. Although my aunt often made incisions in my uncle's skull, he never bore any malice. He woke up quiet and obedient, and sat for many hours among his pigeons, playing them sweet songs, to atone for his neglect.

One day, when my uncle had not had anything to drink— not even his white wine—he got up and extended his arms at full length and bolted through the door before my aunt could stop him. We went outside the house and stood watching him race down the hill, his arms flapping, flying like a bird possessed. After he was out of earshot he dropped his arms but continued to run.

"This is indeed a strange thing," I said, in deep perplexity. "Are you worried, Aunt?"

"No, no," my aunt said. "He is off to the *posada*, that is all. He has not been in a tavern for a long period. This departure is justifiable. One cannot resent it."

My aunt was a fair-minded—a reasonable woman. "You can't have a mule without a sire or a husband without a fault," she would say. "Your uncle is a lazy fool of a man with the belly of a toper, but he has the joy of living, and that is not to be purchased in shops." Although she was often angry with my uncle, I knew that such anger did not signify. It did not reach down to her core. There were times, however, when she became cool and her face was as wooden as a box, and I could not tell then whether she was angry or not. These were the times when my uncle was off with his women.

2

On my twelfth birthday I was to have a pair of shoes. It had been arranged for months. My aunt gave my uncle the money, and my uncle said good-bye to his pigeons collectively, and individually to the Black Devil and the Young Devil. Then he took me round to the back of the pigeon-loft and dug up a little white linen bag which he slipped into his pocket.

"What is that, Uncle?" I asked.

"Nothing. A trifle. A talisman. Let us walk with celerity."

"You have money there, Uncle," I said.

"Pouf, pouf," my uncle said. "Let us talk of your shoes. When I was your age I had not clapped eyes on a single shoe, let alone owned a whole pair. What colour of shoes do you fancy?"

"Red. At least, the heels must be red. Where did you get the money, Uncle?"

"Confidentially," my uncle said, "I saved it. It is my private hoard, and I rely on you not to tell your aunt of it. I saved this money for an occasion."

If you removed the hills it would be five *kilometros* from our house to the Street. With the hills, of course, it was farther. The Street was a thriving village of 300 persons population, but we always called it the Street. This was not because we did not know any better, but because of the arrangement of the village, which was mainly in the form of one street.

When we arrived at the Street it was time to eat. It was obligatory when travelling, my uncle said, to take one's dinner to a tavern, so we entered the *posada* and sat down in one of the compartments. My uncle ordered wine, and I opened up our dinner tins.

In one tin we had *gaz pacho* (cold soup). In the other tin we had rye bread and goat's cheese and chick peas and boneless partridges, which are potatoes cooked in their jackets and rubbed in garlic, very sweet. We also had a *jalluyo*, a special cake in which my aunt had mixed not only flour and olive-oil and sesame seed, but also sugar; and lastly, because it was my birthday, there was a real egg, hard-boiled, not a pigeon's egg, you understand, but an egg laid by a proper domestic fowl. My uncle would not touch this. This delicacy, he said, was entirely for me.

After we had dined I returned the remnants to the tin and sat waiting for my uncle. My uncle was drinking brandy with the father of Carlota Nunez. He was an important man; he owned the *posada*, but you would never have thought it. He sat in his shirt and laughed loudly and slapped my uncle on the back. At first they had taken the brandy by the glass, but my uncle knocked over the glasses and broke them, so then they drank from *cuartillas*. A woman came in and sat down on the edge of the table and my uncle spoke to her. "How are you, wifie?" he said.

"*Asi, asi.* So, so. How are you, old frog?"

"I am in condition," my uncle said. "What would you like best to drink in a wine-glass?" When my uncle said this I kicked him under the table, and he made a number of gestures indicating his surprise and innocence. "Surely," he said. "It is permitted surely that I offer the woman a glass of wine?"

I looked at the woman doubtfully, whereupon she smiled, and I saw that she was not altogether a common woman, for she had gold in her teeth. She was fat and had streaked hair, partly blonde. Her frock was black and adequate, although admittedly there was lace across her breast.

"*Miré,*" my uncle said to the woman, "look here, give her your *manton de mantilla.* Give her your veil, to peer through."

"Don't suck it then," the woman said, handing me the veil.

"There would be no harm perhaps in a single glass," I said.

Soon there were many people in the *posada* and a great clattering of tongues. I had to pull my uncle's sleeve to attract his notice. "It is time to go to the shoe-shop, Uncle," I said.

"I disagree," my uncle said. "The shoe-maker will be engaged in his siesta."

I watched everything, but mostly I watched my uncle and the woman and the shadows cast by the sun. I waited till the shadows of men in the doorway were longer than the men themselves, then I spoke to my uncle again.

"Later," my uncle said. "Later."

Some men carried the father of Carlota Nunez up to his bed, and her mother came to serve customers in the shop. When she had served everybody, she sat down on a wine-cask and mopped her face with a cloth, and I went over and sat down beside her.

"What is the matter, Francesca?" she said.

"*Nada*," I said. "Nothing. I am tired of waiting only. It is my birthday, and my uncle is going to buy me shoes."

"Merciful weather," said Carlota's mother, "it is too late for buying. The shops are all closed, Chicken."

She was a kind woman, and I knew she would not lie to me. I went across to my uncle and punched him with my fist on the chest. My uncle had his arm round the woman's waist and the woman had her head on my uncle's shoulder. I no longer cared for her. Plainly, it was not real gold in her teeth.

"Witness what you have done!" I shouted. "The shops are now closed."

"Go away!" my uncle said. "*Vaya!* Go away home!"

"Uncle," I said, "I am bitterly disappointed with you," and I picked up the dinner tins and went home.

It was late when I got to the house. It was dark and I was tired. My aunt was sitting close to the fire with her shawl over her shoulders. I shut the door and she watched me with narrow eyes. "Well?" she said.

"Well," I said, "he's at it again."

"Drink?"

"That," I said, "and women too." I told her what had happened.

"This woman," my aunt said, "she was *rubia*, blonde, you declare? Had she also one evil eye, slightly?"

"Indeed, yes."

"And had she honey in her hips?"

"Much honey," I said. I showed my aunt how the woman walked. "And gold in her teeth, artificially."

"I know the one," my aunt said calmly. "I know the *rubia*. That *puta!* God grant that she stick her foot in a deep hole and pull out only the stocking!"

"God grant simultaneously," I said, "that she get such a hell of a fever that her bones will pour out in hot soup!"

"Amen," said my aunt. "Now get thee into the bed."

The following day, as was to be expected, my uncle did not come home. And on the next day he did not come neither. Nor on the next. On the morning of the fourth day my aunt said, "We will roast this gander," and she filled a dinner tin and put on her *mantilla* that smelled of moth-balls, and we went down to the Street.

We passed the *posada* and my aunt disdained it. She looked neither to right nor left, and we marched all the way up the Street to the jail. "Inside," my aunt said, pushing me, and we went in.

Señor Garcias, the policeman who officiated in our district, was sitting at his desk smoking a cigar. His desk was covered with papers and nutshells. He was a big, dirty man, a bachelor, too young, my uncle once said, for so much importance.

"Mariqua !" he said, surprised, using my aunt's diminutive. "Indeed now, Mariqua !"

"Note this," my aunt declared. "My man has been three days and three nights with La Rubia."

"I know," Señor Garcias said. "I know all about it." He took his cigar out of his mouth, looked at it, put it back in his mouth, and scratched his head. I perceived that he was afraid of my aunt. "It's a bad business, Mariqua."

"It is not to be tolerated," my aunt said. "Plainly, no. That is why I am present. I have decided to have him incarcerated."

"Well, now," Señor Garcias said, and he laid down his cigar on the edge of the table and scratched himself here and there unhappily. "Well now, Maria, it is not so simple as that. In fact, it is worse than difficult. Bluntly, it is impossible !"

"Impossible !" my aunt said, incredulous. "Is there then no room in the jail ?"

"It is not that. It is a matter of law. It is all here in the book.

Look, you can see the book for yourself. See how thick it is. I cannot go outside the book. I would truly, if I could. *Lo siento mucho.* I am very sorry, I am powerless."

"*Por dio,*" said my aunt, "is there then no justice in the world?"

"It is deeply regretted, Maria."

My aunt turned while he spoke and marched out. She went so fast that I had to run to overtake her.

"I will do what I can," Señor Garcias called after us. "Rest assured that I have your interests at heart, Maria."

"Auntie," I said, "I did not know that you were acquainted with Señor Garcias."

"When I was unmarried he wished to marry me," my aunt said, snapping.

We walked in silence for some miles.

"He is very dirty," I remarked.

"He is a poltroon," my aunt said. "Poor steer of a man, afraid of a book!"

Next morning my uncle came home. I heard afterwards that Señor Garcias had ordered him out of the Street. He came home and jumped into the bed and pulled the blankets up over his head. My aunt said not a word. My uncle lay in bed all day, ignored, eating from the pot when my aunt was out. In the evening he poked his head up clear of the blankets and whispered to me.

"Frasquita!" he said. "The shoes are under the bed."

"The shoes!" I said. I was so surprised that I stood simply, staring.

"Well, look at them!" my uncle said.

"Oh, Uncle," I said, looking. "Uncle, they're beautiful. Truly, I have never seen such beauty in any pair of articles."

They were exactly what I wanted. They were black shoes and

they had red heels and each heel was as long as my thumb. They lacked perfection in one respect only. They were not so large as my feet.

3

Two days later my uncle, still in disgrace, was sitting against the pigeon-loft playing lamentable music to his birds when the train passed in the valley. My uncle watched the train closely, as was his habit, and saw a piece of machinery fall off it. He went down into the valley and retrieved this piece of machinery and brought it up to the house. Although my aunt was not speaking to my uncle she was listening, and when my uncle came and told us of this piece of machinery my aunt and I both went out to the yard to examine it.

"It is evidently of importance," my uncle said. He walked all round it, strutting. "Note the workmanship of the edges. Note the excessive artistry of the letters."

My aunt and I noted, as told. This object was a long white strip of wood—a board—and on it were printed letters.

"It is of primary importance," my uncle said. "No doubt the train is already stopped, incapacitated, for lack of this vital part. I must take it to the Street without delay."

"What do the words say?" my aunt said to me.

"Yes. Read it to us," my uncle said.

I read out the printed words.

DEATH TO THE FAITH. CREATE THE SOVIETS.

"Behold that!" my uncle said. "Can you now doubt its significance! Here are hundreds of travellers sitting innocent upon their bottoms while the train rushes to death and destruction for lack of this integral part. Death," he said. "It says so, in writing. It is clearly imperative that I take this machinery to the Street forthwith."

My aunt and I looked at each other. We did not understand the meaning of the printed words, and we did not think my uncle understood them either.

"Clearly," my uncle said in a loud voice, waiting for my aunt to give him permission, "it is imperative."

My aunt touched the edge of the board with her foot and walked round and surveyed its back. I saw the horn of the dilemma on which she was impaled. She did not wish my uncle to go to the Street, but she was anxious to do what was right.

"Tell him he is to come straight back," she said at last.

I told my uncle.

"*Pronto,*" my uncle said. "Like a ball that bounces. Tell her I promise it."

"He will come straight back," I said to my aunt. "He promises."

"All right, all right, I heard," my aunt said, angry. "These are good ears, not cauliflowers, on my head."

My uncle took up the board and went down to the Street, but he did not come straight back. He did not come back that day. Nor that night. On the afternoon of the following day Manuolo, the blacksmith's boy, who was noted for his memory and commonly employed as a reciter, came to recite a message to my aunt. The words of the message were as follows: "From Señor Garcias, *Polizonte* to Maria, wife of Federico. Your old man is in jail, as requested, for political reasons, until you want that he should be released. It is expected that you will feed him as from noon to-morrow. In eternal obedience. A. GARCIAS."

My aunt nodded, pleased. "That is good," she said, and she took Manuolo into the house and gave him wine from her own skin and some *churros,* oil fritters. When Manuolo rose to go away she stopped him. "One moment," she said. "Here, take this down to him in the jail." And she gave the boy my uncle's *bandurria.* "One will now have more space for living," she explained to me.

The following day, as was the custom when my uncle was in the jail, I took his food and a basket containing four pigeons to the Street. My uncle was then able to acquaint us with his requirements by despatching a pigeon with one of the following messages appended to its leg:

"X"

"XX"

"XXX"

"XXXX"

This was my uncle's method of writing, and was such that even my aunt could read it. One cross meant that my uncle wanted more food. Two crosses meant that he wanted more wine. Three crosses indicated that he had perceived by instinct that either the Black Devil or the Young Devil required attention, and four crosses meant that we were to come quickly, my uncle was dying. This was an urgent message and naturally my uncle did not send it often. In truth, we did not attach significance to my uncle's messages, however urgent, because even when he had no requirements he despatched all four pigeons with messages each day. It pleased him to do this because of the importance of such behaviour. Naturally, none of the others in the jail had such a convenience: it elevated him above them all.

Usually when my uncle was in jail I climbed the lemon tree in order to view him and to converse over the courtyard wall, but my aunt made it clear to me, using the double negative for emphasis, that on this occasion I was not to speak with my uncle. Not on any account. So I handed the food pail and the basket to Señor Garcias, and ate my own dinner on the side of the hill, and then went home.

On the humpback bridge I met Sara Cortez, who is thirteen and a woman. "Good day, Francesca," she said. "Well, what of this now? I hear you are to be rich."

"Explain it to me if you please," I said.

"Strangers have been to your house," she informed me. "The Mayor's brother from a city and one other. They went laden with money-bags to buy a pigeon. I dare say you will be evident in a new dress and as grand as anybody now."

"Sara, not the Black Devil! Truly, they have not purchased that particular bird!"

"What other?" Sara said.

I ran all the rest of the way home. There was lubrication neither in my mouth nor in the inside of my stomach. The inside of my stomach felt terrible.

My aunt was carrying a tub of rock salt to the pigeon-loft, and when she saw me she laid down the tub and knotted her hands together on her chest. "Whatever it is I can bear it, please God," she said. "Now withdraw the tongue into thy mouth and speak."

"Auntie," I said. "Auntie, you have not sold the Black Devil!"

"Is this all the fuss?"

I nodded. I could see my aunt's thoughts moving in the back of her eyes, and I no longer needed an answer. I knew that all was well. I sat down on an ant-heap, I was so out of breath, and wept.

"To be sure you are an excellent one!" my aunt said, surveying me. "One does not expect milk from a calf of your maturity, but neither does one expect water. Plug thy leaks and discontinue this exhibition. If you would know, I have despatched these *caballeros* with stern and dirty words, to match their dealing. Now pray assist me with the rock salt."

I could not stop my sniffling. "I knew you would never sell the Devil, Auntie," I said.

"I have no love for the birds," my aunt said, staggering with the tub, "on account of their big bellies. But this concerns honour. Manifestly it is not a matter of buying and selling."

That night it rained. That was Tuesday. The next day also it rained. When the sun set it stopped raining. When the sun rose it started again to rain. And it continued like this each day and night. It was most inconvenient. On the Saturday morning my aunt said, "No more. We have had too much. You are tired of wetting your clothes and I am tired of drying your clothes. And it is bad for the material. I shall go today to the Street, in person. I shall confer with Señor Garcias and I shall liberate your uncle. Do you agree with this programme of action?"

"I agree unanimously," I said, "in the circumstances."

My aunt went, alone, to the village. I remained in the home, attending to the duties. I fed the pigeons, cleaned the room, and made an arrangement of objects to my satisfaction. In the afternoon I slept like an adult, then I put the *puchero*, the stew, on the fire and scrubbed the table and placed the spoons. I went frequently to look down into the valley for my kin, i.e. my uncle and my aunt, and when I saw them, as small as two finger-nails in the anatomy of the lowland, I went and took the milk from the goats and, returning, adjusted the room, establishing order. I took off my bag dress and put on my frock and my apron, then I went to meet my uncle and my aunt.

My aunt was walking fast, bent slightly forward like a racer. My uncle was walking a step behind, carrying his *bandurria*.

When he saw me he threw back his shoulders and began to whistle, but he had to walk faster than his swaggering speed to keep up with my aunt and thus did not look at ease, despite.

To eat, we had *sopa de arroz*, rice soup, and the stew, and bread and goat's cheese, and I must say it was excellent. My uncle said I was a cook of distinction and that the meal was fit for him. My uncle was extremely merry, watching my aunt's face and my face, bursting into snatches of song, making many of his old jokes in new ways, and talking without cessation. My aunt said little, and nothing to my uncle, but after we were in bed she began on him. Truly, I had not realised my aunt. I had not known of her wind-bag.

"All right," my uncle would say. "All right, I have promised. I have made my mark on the official paper which says positively that I will not have dealings with this woman again. What further proof of my innocence can be required?"

"Your innocence! I admire that!"

"My future innocence," my uncle said with dignity. "My future innocence is not to be questioned."

My aunt would not be checked. She continued and continued. So much talk was unseemly from a silent woman. Formerly, one had attached so much value to her words that now one could not disregard them. They pounded, each one, against us like hard, bony fists.

Finally, my uncle sat up in the bed and reached over and picked me up and laid me between my aunt and him. This was revolutionary, for we always lay in the order of getting up, my uncle in the inside of the bed, then my aunt, then me.

"Now let there be peace," my uncle said.

He lay with his back to me, and my aunt lay with her back to me, and I lay on my back between them. But despite this my aunt did not cease to speak. Sometimes she would stop for several minutes, and I would close my eyes and my uncle would breathe loudly as if he were sleeping, then my aunt, with her back to us, would recommence all over again. It was most improper behaviour. One could deduce from it how angry my aunt was. She was giving my uncle his last chance. This was made quite clear.

I had not said anything at all, not a word, but at last I said in an angry voice: "Would you kindly inform me how I am to sleep?"

"Yes," my uncle said. "Tell us, how is the child to get her sleep?"

"Hold your tongue, Uncle," I said. "Both of you. As for you, my aunt, if you open your mouth again I shall put my foot in it."

There was silence then, and my aunt said nothing more, but, except for my uncle, we did not sleep for a long time.

4

For many weeks thereafter my uncle's behaviour was an example to all mankind. He did not get up in the mornings, of course, but he assisted with the vines, carried water, milked the goats, and even repaired the aged hole in the roof. He did everything that my aunt told him. No sooner had she given him an order three or four times than it got done. The stiffness went out of my aunt's manner, my uncle became important again, and there was much for us all to laugh at. Altogether it was a privilege to live in so well-regulated a home.

This continued for a month, fully, then one day my uncle got out of bed in the morning a.m. He sat down at the table and ate with us.

"*Paloma*," he said to my aunt. This means pigeon, but it was my uncle's nice word for my aunt. "*Paloma*, I am going to the Street. Fill me a tin of food." My uncle said this quite casually, as if it were the custom for him to be bolt upright at breakfast time talking of going to the Street.

My aunt inclined her face, eating, so that you could see only the top of her head.

"I do not wish to go to that malodorous place," my uncle said. "But it is required. I have reason to believe that this is the month of September. It is now necessary for the Notary to inscribe the form of entry so that the Black Devil may race again for the Championship of Andalusia."

"Francesca could attend to the matter," my aunt said, "for this is the day that she is committed to make responses to the priest."

"Impossible," my uncle said. "This is a matter for men. This is *business*."

My aunt did not raise her face.

"I shall therefore require a dinner tin," my uncle said loudly.

"So be it," my aunt said.

My uncle left the house early. "There may be delays," he explained. "In a transaction of this nature there is need for much caution, but you may depend on me, I shall not permit humming and hawing. I shall demand speed, and then I shall come home like an end of elastic."

I remained for an hour assisting my aunt, then I too set out for the Street. In addition to me there were two Street girls making responses, but the priest was plainly in a busy mood and despatched us in a few minutes. "You are clever girls," he said. "You know it all."

I then went and stood at the *posada* door, looking for my uncle. Inside, there were many people, but not my uncle. I next went to the Notary's office. There was a young lady in the office, sitting behind a machine. She had the air of a young lady from a city.

"Has my uncle been?" I said.

She did not know my uncle, and I had to describe my uncle's dimensions and his business.

"He has been and gone," she said. "Your uncle, eh?"

"My only uncle," I said. I did not like her.

I now came to the conclusion that my uncle had left the Street to return home, but in this I erred. It was Carlota Nunez who corrected me. "If you are looking for your uncle," she said, "I saw him standing at the back door of a certain house."

"Was there anybody with him?" I asked.

"No, only La Rubia," Carlota said.

I was exceedingly dismayed.

"You can see the house from where we stand," Carlota said, and she indicated it to me. "If you proceed along the lane you will have a clear view of the back door. That is where your uncle is."

I ran along the lane. I hoped that Carlota was telling lies, for she had told me lies before, but this time it was unmistakably true. My uncle was leaning against the doorway talking to someone. I could not see her, but I could see a portion of her skirt and I could hear her voice. It was La Rubia, indisputably.

When I scuffed my feet on the lane my uncle turned and saw me. He stood upright and straightened his hat and put his hands in his pockets and tried to smile. He did not know what to do with his limbs, including his head. Plainly, he was a guilty man.

"So, Uncle!" I said.

"Now, Francesca, beloved Frasquita," my uncle said, and he walked towards me, making gestures with his hands, arranging a welcome on his face. "Good!" he said. "Excellent. At last I have found you. Splendid. I have explored each section of the Street, and now, happily, I have found you here." While my uncle was speaking he was waggling one hand behind his back to La Rubia. This was a signal for her to close the door and disappear, but she did not have the necessary intelligence to comprehend it. She poked her head round the door and exhibited her gold teeth, saying, "Hullo, little girl." Smiling, the fat cat.

"I have nothing to say to you," I said. "And to you likewise, Uncle, I have nothing to say. But to my aunt when I return home I shall have much to say. Indeed yes." And I walked away.

"Halt, Frasquita!" my uncle said, running after me. "You are entirely in error. I am innocent. Nevertheless, if you inform your aunt she will surely murder me at least. What have you to say to that?"

"It will be a regrettable incident," I said, "but no doubt we can find another man."

"Frasquita!" my uncle said, catching my arm. "Beloved Frasquita, consider my repeated kindnesses. Consider the songs I have taught thee! Consider the shoes with red heels. Consider all the glories I have promised thee. Frasquita, I implore thee!"

These were solemn words, drumming in the ear-hole. An honourable girl could not ignore such words. I stopped and contemplated my uncle.

"Angel of mercy!" my uncle said. "I am now witnessing the true child. Clearly you have decided for honour. You will not tell your aunt. You are about to promise it!"

I looked into my uncle's eyes as an equal.

"I will not tell my aunt," I said, "provided I get her *manton de mantilla*." And I nodded my head in the direction of La Rubia. "I impose that condition."

"But what can a little girl like you want a veil for?"

"I want it for allure," I said, "naturally."

"And you will not tell?"

"I will not tell," I said, "if I get the *manton de mantilla*. I promise it."

My uncle retreated to the house and spoke with La Rubia. They spoke in whispers and I could not hear what was said. After a few minutes La Rubia retired into the house and returned with a veil. My uncle bore it importantly to me. "Here," he said. "Take it. This incomparable article. It is yours, absolutely."

"Wait," I said, and I held the veil up to my face and looked through it. "This does not satisfy me, Uncle. I do not wish to own a discarded veil. I wish that particular veil which La Rubia wore on the 4th of August, last month."

My uncle stared at me.

"The veil that she wore in the *posada*," I said. "That is the one I want. That is the only one which fulfils my conditions."

"The only one?"

"Verily," I said.

My uncle went back and spoke to La Rubia again. On this occasion they spoke for a long time, and when my uncle handed back the old veil La Rubia threw it on the ground and stamped her foot. I walked to the end of the lane and whistled the beginning of an Ave Maria. I was not only nervous but afraid. I was terrified at the dimensions of my sin, but I was even more terrified that I would not obtain the veil. I stood at the end of the lane with my back to my uncle and La Rubia, whistling. Any person seeing me would have thought that I was unconcerned and idling, but really I was praying. I was praying with passion for that veil.

Eventually my uncle approached. He handed me a veil—the

correct, the *posada* veil. "Francesca," he said sadly, "you are a bad girl and I cannot understand it. I do not know where you could have learned such badness living in our saintly home. Nevertheless, you are plainly a little old bad girl, and on this occasion the forces of evil have conquered the forces of good."

I did not attend to him, I was too busy fingering the veil.

"Now you will not tell!" my uncle said. "You have promised."

"I will not tell," I said. "But you are to come home immediately."

"It is out of the question," my uncle said. "I must first placate La Rubia. Be reasonable, Frasquita. She is violently enraged. She is like a bull from whom the outer skin has been removed in its sleep. She might herself go and demand the veil from your aunt."

"In that case," I said, "you may have a half-hour. But no longer. And it is stupid to say she is like a bull, for a bull and a woman are two different matters. Now note, if you are not home a half-hour behind me I shall tell my aunt this entire history, regardless. That is my speech."

My uncle was standing solid on the backs of his heels, regarding me. "You are certainly a little old bad devil of a girl nowadays, Francesca," he said unhappily. He did not understand that I was growing up, that I had learned to treat him with firm hands. I left him in his sad stance and, holding the veil carefully, walked, a stately figure, up the lane. I did not run till I was round the corner, out of my uncle's sight, and then I raced with all my speed.

Out in the valley I ran and skipped and danced. I tried on the veil and sang. "I have a *manton de mantilla*," I sang. "A beautiful real veil of my own." Oh, I was happy! I have rarely seen so much happiness in any one girl. For perfection I required only to see myself in the looking-glass. When I thought of the looking-glass, I thought also of my aunt who owned it, and a sensation manifested itself in my stomach. I decided that I would put the veil in a box and bury it until such time as my uncle won the Championship of the Entire World and provided me with a drawer of my own. Buried was the only safe place for the veil. Anywhere else my aunt would certainly find it.

Approaching the house I hid the veil up the back of my skirt and walked with decorum. I went to the shed behind the pigeon-loft and took out a small box which had served to carry eggs to the Street, and I placed the veil in this box. I took the spade and paced eight steps from the shed, and I dug a hole there and got the box and put it in the hole. I was covering it gently with earth when my aunt came round the side of the pigeon-loft and saw me.

"What is it?" she said. "What is the matter, Francesca?"

I was red as beetroot, at least, and I was dumb. When I tried to speak the result was purely negative. No, nothing came. My aunt bent down and picked up the box and opened it and took out the veil.

"Francesca," she said, "where did you get this veil?"

I could not look at my aunt.

"Francesca!" my aunt said, shouting.

I shook my head.

"Go to the house," my aunt said. In all my life I had not heard my aunt use this particular voice. It was entirely a novelty, and it froze my interior solid. "Precede me to the house at once."

We went into the house, and my aunt closed the door and I stood looking at her feet. "If one had told me with the voice of a saint, I should have said that one lied," my aunt declared. "I would not never have believed that my Francesca was a thief.

Are you now going to tell me from whom you stole it, this article, this costly *manton de mantilla* ?"

I said nothing. I had no power of saying.

"Lie on the bed," my aunt said.

I lay on the bed with my nose pushed hard into the blanket and my bottom up, ready. I hoped that my nose would break. I lay on my hot face, waiting, and millions of noises in my ears.

"Thou to thieve !" my aunt said.

I waited for a long time. When nothing happened, I looked between my legs with one eye, and saw that my aunt was sitting at the table, weeping.

"That thou shouldst thieve !" she whispered.

"I did not thieve it, Auntie !" I said. I was weeping myself now. "I did not, I did not !" I had seen my aunt with tears in her eyes, but never before had I seen her abandoned to weeping. She was no longer angry. The hardness had gone out of her, and all her sharp angles were curved and drooping. That was the terrible thing. "Truly, truly, Auntie," I said, and I ran to her and hid my face in her lap, and she put her hand on my head and I told her the whole history then.

My aunt did not say anything for a very long time, but I felt the stiffness returning to her bones. "Enough of this folly," she said at last, and she slapped the back of my neck. "We have a serious affair on our hands. It is necessary to terminate your uncle's habits for truly the last time. If he is obedient he will be here soon. We must hasten. Go and fetch the Black Devil. I have decided on it."

"The Black Devil !" I said, lifting my head and staring. "What are you going to do, Auntie ?"

"Verily," my aunt said, "a bird in the pot is worth a hundred flying. Get the Devil."

"No !" I said. "No, no, Auntie. Some other bird."

"No other bird," my aunt said sharply. "The Devil. Go and fetch him."

I could not do it and I could not bear to see it done. When my aunt herself went to the pigeon-loft I left the house and ran with velocity till I came to the stream and could run no farther. Then I lay on the sloping moss with my hands full of it and seriously wished that I was dead. This was my first experience of tragedy on a large scale, and I was not now the same girl that I had been in the morning. I was no longer a girl at all. The pain in my heart was the size of an adult's, at least. I lay for a long time, long enough for my aunt to have plucked and roasted the corpse, and for my uncle to have returned and eaten it, then I went slowly back to the house.

My aunt was standing looking down into the valley. There she was, fixed, like a statue. Hearing me, she turned and nodded her head. "He is coming," she said, and together, without speaking, we entered the house. I kept my face averted from the fireplace. I studied the toes of my left foot and listened with both my ears. I was very frightened, and my aunt too was frightened: her movements were entirely unusual.

"We ought not to have done it, Auntie," I said.

My aunt opened and closed the oven door, making much noise, then she arranged the eating implements for a second time.

"I am scared, Auntie," I said. "Something terrible may happen. My uncle may even hack you with the axe. He is a very passionate man."

"That is undeniable," my aunt said. "But he is also a reasonable man, when sober. He understands justice, I hope."

"Nevertheless, I wish we had not done it."

"Chist now!" my aunt said. "He is coming closely!"

My uncle came in whistling. He walked to the fire and

warmed his rear and spoke to us in jocular terms. An exhausting day, he declared. A day of intricate paper-work. "There is no other thing like documents," he said, "to tire a man. Hey-ho, behold the stiffness of my wrist. But eventually the business was concluded, and I now take pleasure in announcing to you that the Black Devil is entered and that our fortunes are again assured."

My aunt brushed past him and opened the oven-door and withdrew the unrecognisable body of the Black Devil. I did not look.

"Ha!" my uncle said. "Quail. Good!" And he rubbed his hands together and sat down at his place. The truth could not occur to him, because in our house we did not ever eat the pigeon. "Excellent," he said. "But is it only a single quail?"

"We have previously eaten," my aunt said, her voice strange.

"Well, well," my uncle said. "It is a long time since I have satisfied myself with quail. Did we receive this gift presumably from the wife of Redhand Garcias?"

My aunt did not reply, and my uncle picked up the bird and tore it asunder and began to eat. I watched fascinated. I did not want to watch, but my eyes were fixed. It was a fearful spectacle.

"Good," my uncle said, his mouth full of the priceless bird. He looked up and saw me and nodded, winking. "Very good," he said. "Exquisite. Although one must mention, truly, that it is not a youthful bird. *Qué pasa?* What is the matter with you, Francesca?"

I could not speak, and when my uncle put an entire leg in his mouth, crunching, I could not bear it any longer. I could not simply contain my emotion, and I clapped my hands over my mouth and began to cry.

"Women!" my uncle said, and he bit hard into the bone. He looked at me searchingly, to see if I had told, and then he looked at my aunt. My aunt was standing by the fire, rigid, her breasts drawn up, her hands clasped in front of her and the bones showing through her flesh everywhere. My uncle took the leg out of his mouth and surveyed it, then he addressed himself to my aunt. "What is the matter?" he demanded, his eyes shifting quickly from my aunt to me and back to my aunt again. "Speak up, woman. Is it some fatality? Is it sickness among the birds?"

My aunt said nothing. Still staring, my uncle put the leg back in his mouth. "It could not possibly concern the Black Devil?" he said.

I closed my eyes. "Have mercy, God!" I said.

The next thing there was an explosion inside my uncle's mouth and he cast his chair aside and ejected himself through the door like a shot rabbit.

"He has gone to the pigeons," I said. "Oh, Auntie, what will happen to us now?"

"It will be all right, it will be all right," my aunt whispered. I think she could not produce a bigger voice. She was trembling like a machine, you could hear her, and her face was fit for the shroud. I put my fingernails into the flesh that was nearest and bled, and did not know it. And we just stood, and waited, and listened.

After a long, long time we heard the door of the pigeon-loft. We heard my uncle's steps on the path, only they did not sound like the steps of my uncle, or any girl's uncle, they sounded like the steps of a giant.

At last he entered.

He had no weapon in his hands, and he did not look angry and he did not look surprised. He did not look anything. He sat down. You would not credit it. He sat ordinarily down and pushed the plate away from him.

"Well," he said. "Well, am I to have no food, woman?"

My aunt became animated with movement, and I too moved, helping her. We filled up a plate of stew and placed it before my uncle.

"Bread," my aunt said. She cut the bread and put it in my uncle's hand. "And you too," she said to me. "You will eat now."

"And you also, Auntie," I said.

"We shall all eat," my aunt said.

My uncle did not speak, and my aunt and I did not speak. We ate entirely in silence, my uncle small and sorrowful, and my aunt just eating and me watching them both. Then my aunt finished eating and stood up and began to lift the dishes. She addressed herself suddenly to my uncle.

"You still possess the Young Devil," she said.

My uncle was not expecting speech, and it seemed that the words took a long time to reach him. His head jerked at last like the head of a startled horse, and he said, "No!" shouting. "No, no, you would not . . . I beseech you! . . . you could not do it, *mujer*!"

"I have not declared for doing anything," my aunt said. "I have made a statement, simply. I have said that you still possess the Young Devil, and that is plainly true," and she walked out.

My uncle put his arms on the table and hid his face in his arms and wept. A revolution was in progress. A great change was taking place in my family, and in all of us within the family, but I did not know of it until my uncle raised his head and spoke.

"One must allow for her," he said. "Your aunt is a very passionate woman, Francesca."

CASE OF MISS WARING

CASEBOOK. WORKING NOTES

Strictly Private

JANUARY 6. R.G. BIRDMAN TO SEE ME TODAY. WANTS ME TO examine fiancée, dancer apparently (Ballet). See name in Appts. Book. R.G. interrupted during session with F. Samson says she told him I was engaged, but that he insisted on walking into my room. Particularly irritating, because I was on the point of beginning transference with F., who is one of the most difficult cases I have had. And, of course, after Birdman came blundering in, she closed up like a clam.

January 10. Birdman again at 2 p.m. He hasn't changed much in the past twelve years. Fatter, of course, and more pompous than ever. Obviously prosperous. Told me something about a legacy, and seemed surprised that I didn't know. Very friendly, repeatedly calling me Johnny. Why? Never did at school as far as I can remember. Attitude objectionable, but so unconscious that I didn't bother to pull him up. Saying in effect, you and I know very well that psycho-analysis is a racket, but just in case there may sometimes be something in it, I want you to give my fiancée a course of treatment, and, mind you, it must be the best, the Very First-class treatment for V.I.P.s. I explained carefully that I could not accept his fiancée until I had examined her and decided whether she was a suitable subject for analysis, and that if I did so decide, the treatment would be an orthodox course, the same as everyone else got, and that this course would last for several months and might extend over years. R.G. slightly deflated. "You must take her," he said. "It's vital. You see, I think she's a schizo."

"I beg your pardon," I said.

"You know," he said. "A schizophrenic. I'm almost certain of it."

I was amused but said nothing. R.G. has obviously been reading up his psychiatry, but has not read quite enough. If the girl really is a schizo, I won't touch the case, of course.

"I'm damnably worried," R.G. said.

Went on to tell me that they were to be married this year, but as the girl (Jill) is young, twenty-one, he is quite prepared to wait. At the same time hinted pretty broadly that in view of the fact that we went to school together, he expected me to curtail *the cure*. ("I know how reluctant you chaps are to let a patient go, but if you make a quick job of Jill you won't lose by it financially if you know what I mean.")

I knew only too well what he meant. What a bounder the fellow is! Decided definitely not to accept the girl and therefore did not press him for her symptons. Strikes me now as odd, however, that he did not volunteer symptoms. As he was leaving, asked me not to mention to fiancée, whom I am seeing in half an hour, that he (R.G.) had called a second time. Miss Samson heard the last few minutes of our conversation at the door, and treated me to the smile matronly and sympathetic as I returned to my room. Samson is no mean psychologist.

Jill Waring. Native of Leith. Member of *corps de ballet*—Faméchon-Lisle, now at Queen's.

Only child.

Age 22. (Check: Birdman told me 21, and this may be a straw in the wind.)

5 ft. 5 in. approx. Wt. 115 lb. (apparently constant).

Good appearance, neat and tidy, figure noticeable. Brunette. Blue eyes. Pupils large but similar. Hair up. Good head. Slightly distended nostrils. Carefully and, I think, expensively dressed. Very attractive.

Handshake normal.

Temperature normal.

Headache and sleeplessness. "Not concentrating quite so well as I used to." Persistent "neuralgia" (!) in left thigh. These are the only symptoms meantime admitted.

No defect of attention or lack of coherence in speech.

Visual and aural perception normal.

Reasoning and judgment—normal reaction to Franz's advanced test.

Appears willing to co-operate, although obviously on the defensive.

Name of family doctor: Brown-Hughes, 186, Clinton Gdns. 54217.

Slight tendency to frown and odd occasional uplift of eyes. (Conjunctivitis?) Arrange eye test.

Smoked three cigarettes in half an hour. Holds cigarette in left hand.

Crossed and uncrossed legs repeatedly. Tendency to carelessness with skirt, which may be due to stage casualness, but which does not accord with general air of fastidiousness.

Took writing sample before she left, primarily to get gloves off. Good strong backhand. Hands large for a woman. Long sensitive fingers. After we had shaken hands I tried experiment of G.H.C.'s. Don't like this sort of thing, as it savours of a bag of tricks, but can be useful. I said, "Do you always have a secretion of sweat on the palm of your hand?" and she said, "Yes, usually," very quickly. The interesting thing was that I had not detected sweat.

Too early for any conclusions. I know nothing yet, but interesting because one seldom gets an opportunity, as seems probable in this case, of *preventive* psycho-therapy.

January 11. Rang Brown-Hughes early evening. Knew I was going to have trouble directly I heard his voice. And I did. I understood he had recently given the girl a thorough examination, and I asked him if he would be good enough to give me the facts.

B.-H. What facts?

Self. Oh, just the usual. In the first place, is there anything organically wrong?

B.-H. I don't keep records of these routine examinations.

Self. Well, can you remember if there was any abnormality?

B.-H. Of course I remember. There was none.

Self. What about the patient's history?

B.-H. What about it?

Self. Will you give me an outline, please?

B.-H. What do you want to know?

Self. Everything of interest. Beginning at the beginning, what about the birth? Can you remember if there was any difficulty, if it was a forceps birth, for instance?

B.-H. Good God Almighty, etc.

Self. All right, Doctor. I just thought you might remember. How about childhood illnesses? Meningitis, concussion, fainting attacks, rheumatic fever, chorea?

B.-H. None of 'em.

Self. And the family history?

B.-H. Mother was all right.

Self. What about the father?

B.-H. So-so.

Self. What do you mean by that?

B.-H. Oh . . . normal.

Self. And the grandparents?

B.-H. Before my time.

Self. I heard the grandfather was inclined to be eccentric.

B.-H. Well, that's one way of putting it.

Self (exhausted). Look here, I'd like to come and see you. When could I come? This is important, Doctor.

B.-H. It's not important to me.

Self. It's important to your patient.

We argued about this for several minutes, B.-H. becoming profane, and I had to turn on my big guns, bringing in the names of Professors H. and S., and stating that I would have to hold him responsible for any deterioration in the patient's condition.

"The patient has no condition," he shouted. But in the end he gave me an hour next week. "Provided you're qualified. I won't see you unless you're qualified. Are you?"

"I have the same degrees as you have yourself, Doctor," I said. And I forbore to add that I also had two others. I don't want to score points off the miserable old sod. I want facts.

I should be amused, I suppose. G.H.C. would make a wonderful story of it. Blimp to end all Drs. Blimp. The trouble is there are so many B.-H.s. The G.P.s should be solidly behind us, and they're not. And why blame the P.B.G.P.? The specialists are just as bad. Obstruction all the way. How can we possibly get results when the profession as a whole is concerned only to prove us charlatans, and God knows that's easy enough. I'm tired tonight and I'm worried about V. Talking far too much today. I think he is going to have another breakdown, which will make his son's gratitude seem excessive, to say the least of it. Trouble is, I sent the £250 to the clinic, so can't very well return it to him.

Birdman rang and told me he'd rung twice already this afternoon, but couldn't get me. I snapped, telling him I had other patients as well as his fiancée. Birdman is going to be a nuisance. Told him I didn't know yet whether I'd be able to help her or not, but that I expected to be able to say definitely after two or three sessions whether I'd accept her as a patient.

Birdman then became very inarticulate and wordy, and I gathered that he was in the process of telling me something. He went round and round it. "I hardly like to tell you on the telephone," he said at last.

"Well, don't tell me."

"I might as well," he said. "I don't suppose there'll be anybody listening. You see, it's like this, she's . . . well, I don't know any other way to put it, Johnny. . . . She's man crazy."

This case is going to be trickier than I had thought.

January 20. Went to the ballet again last night. *Cotillon.* Think I am getting the hang of the thing. Lack of story bothers me a bit though.

January 28. I spent all last evening going over Samson's verbatim notes of my week's work, with especial reference to V. Not concentrating perfectly. There is something escaping me with regard to Jill W., and this is lying at the back of my mind and coming between me and my insight into V.

Can't make up my mind about this verbatim business. I know it isn't recommended, and I know all the reasons why, but I'm sure that in my case it has done far more good than harm to have someone in the next room taking a word-for-word record. It would ruin my relationship with any patient who realised it, of course, but I can rule out the possibility of a patient ever finding out. What it does to Samson really doesn't matter. Samson is just the stooge. What *does* matter is what it does to me. Does it tighten me up, can it possibly communicate itself in some degree through me to the patient? I have felt recently that I am coming against stronger resistances than ever before, and I must consider whether this is due to some positiveness in myself brought about by the fact that I know Samson is over-hearing. Against this I have to bear in mind that I have picked up a great deal that I would otherwise have missed by studying Samson's notes. I find I can now re-experience both visually and aurally every minute of each sitting. Tiring but valuable. E.g. Jill's, "The reason I didn't want to put my hair up was because then I would have to wash my ears every day. I didn't want to be so aware of them."

Self. But you wear your hair up now.

Jill. Oh *yes*.

It was the inflexion that gave that answer such significance, and I quite missed it the first time. . . .

Another danger about the verbatim method is that it further promotes my tendency to lay too much stress on the spoken word. Speech is important, of course. Foremost medium of communication, basis of all my work, etc., etc., but it's not all-important, and I know that I am sometimes misled by attributing shades of meaning that are not intended or even understood by the patients. I must not be so damned subtle about words. Find that I now tend to reproduce even personal conversations verbatim. E.g. my conversation with L. as I drove her home last night. Found myself playing it off after-wards in bed like a gramophone record. No harm in this, of

course, but what *is* dangerous is that in those repeat performances I am lifting the needle at every second word and
subjecting it to far too close a scrutiny. People do not use
words precisely, and by interpreting words too precisely I am
apt to misinterpret the speaker's meaning, which is of course
all that matters: N.B. this.

Jill W. at 3 p.m. Shadows under both eyes.

Still exhibiting all the signs of resistance. Keeps turning to
look at me. Asks questions, and when I do not answer pouts most
disarmingly. Reaction time poor at free association. Started off
by saying, "I have nothing at all to say today. I feel empty."

I waited, and when nothing more came I said, "I think I
noticed you smoothing your hair back over your forehead. Why
did you do this?"

"Because a few hairs had come loose."

"All right," I said. "Start from there. Free association. Hair."

"Hair," she said (3 seconds). "Tights are absurdly dear. I had
to pay six guineas for a pair of chequered tights for *Cotillon*,
and the same thing exactly is advertised in Benjie's pre-war
catalogue at twenty-seven and sixpence."

Nothing more.

"Benjie," I said.

"Twenty-seven and sixpence."

I waited for fully five seconds. "What is the connection
between hair and tights?"

"I have hairy legs," she said. "Haven't you noticed?"

Nothing more.

"Why don't you ever reply?" she asked, sitting up. "Why
don't you try to help me? You just sit there where I can't even
see you and listen and watch me. I feel you watching me all the
time. It's a horrid feeling. Why don't you do something
positive to help?"

Promising outburst, but no more.

"I'll tell you why, Miss Waring," I said. "The answer is very simple. I don't know how to help you." And I reminded her of the explanation of analysis which I had given her when she first came to me. I stressed again that in the early stages it was she who had to do all the work, and that latterly it was possible that I might be able to take a more active part; but that meantime, if the analysis was going to be successful, she must break down her resistances and be honest with me. "You're really the doctor," I said. (Foolish. Have remarked this before. *No* metaphors to patients.) "I'm just the instrument. . . ."

"You're the knife," she said.

"All right, go on from there. Free association. Knife."

"Knife. Scalpel. Dissection. I do not want to be dissected. (*Note:* do not. Normally says, don't). Not today. I'm not in the mood. I had a bad night. I don't want any more today. Anyway, I feel all right. There's nothing really the matter with me, is there? Is there, Doctor?"

Said nothing.

"You might as well answer, because I'm really not going to endure a session today. I feel fine. You don't think there's really anything the matter, do you?"

Had that one many times before, and it's a teaser. Say you don't think there's much the matter and it's a 2 to 1 chance on resentment. Say you think there's something the matter and you increase anxiety neurosis. Text-book answer is, "I don't know. That's what we are trying to find out."

She was putting on her gloves. "Anyway," she said. "I meant to tell you we have an early rehearsal today. And you still haven't answered my question. You don't think there's anything much the matter with me, do you?"

"Yes," I said, "I do."

"You're right, of course," she said. Thought she was going to cry, and that might have helped. She didn't though. "You're always right," she said after a pause. "What am I going to do?"

I said, "You're going to lie back and relax for a moment or two and then we'll begin again."

"All right," she said, "if you'll pull down the blind a little farther."

(The blind again. We've had the blind at least once a sitting.)

Now take the above. Knife stuff on the surface, grist to the mill. Good phallic phenomena. Only too good, and misleading, if disassociated from patient's attitude and expression, which was then and is repeatedly mischievous; this despite the fact that a few moments previously she was showing a genuine emotion. Am almost sure that this is not negative transference or even initial resistance in the ordinary sense. This is not id. work, but pure ego. Deliberate obstructionism. And that brings me to a big problem which has been present from the beginning and which I must presently face up to. Am I right to continue with this patient? Is this perhaps a case where she is too conscious of my personality to be able to use me as a father confessor? Am I too young for her? . . .

Telephone. I knew immediately who it was from Samson's face. "Second time this afternoon," Samson said primly. L. of course. Wants me to join her at N.B. on Friday. Told her I couldn't possibly come down till Saturday as arranged, and reminded her that I was going to the ~~ballet~~ theatre with the B.s. L. becoming possessive. Why is it that I don't resent this? Is it because I'm not particularly good with women in a private capacity that I find their occasional possessiveness flattering to my ego? Or just the normal masc. vanity?

February 7. Long session with R.G.B. Needlessly painful because of the parentheses and rationalisations with which he envelops every relevant fact. Mind is full of cotton-wool, and I was shown most of it. Thinking always, of course, from the conventional, moral point of view, and apparently incapable of ever understanding that this is a cancer like any other and that I am no more interested in his moral attitude than any other surgeon would be while performing a major operation. And a job like this is a major operation. Interview extremely painful for us both, and the sum total that emerged was hardly enough to make a bishop blush. Nevertheless, I suppose to R.G.B. her behaviour seems "pretty shameful" (favourite expression), and if his facts are correct (note the if), and if I am right in thinking also that he toned them down for my consumption, then there is, to put it mildly, a genuine psychoneurosis and a pathological state which certainly should be treated by psychotherapy. Why do I have to argue all this out? I think because I am coming to the same point again: of course, there's psychogenic trouble here, and I've known it all along. The question is, am I competent to relieve it?

These *ifs*. Can't quite correlate R.G.B.'s version of Jill with my own. Have gone into this thoroughly with myself, and am now satisfied that my reluctance to take R.G.B.'s stories at face value is not due to the fact that I do not wish to believe them, but due solely to my conviction that he is not a reliable witness on such matters, being himself morbidly erotic. E.g. he asked me today whether he could attend with Jill, and when I said no, which of course he expected, he asked if he could "listen-in." I said that he couldn't P.D.Q., whereupon bright boy suggested that if it was a matter of the walls being too thick, he could arrange for a house decorator to do the necessary job overnight. He was about to tell me how handsomely he proposed to pay me for this little concession when I shut him up.

"I know," he said. "Everything that you've said is true. It's just that I'm so damned jealous, Johnny."

To revert, I accept what R.G.B. has told me about Jill's erotism in a general way but not in detail. It doesn't match up with my own observations, and I am satisfied that I am not concerned with the fact that it offends my instincts. Although personally I consider R.G.B. unwholesome, I have had clear evidence that Jill does not. On the contrary, she is in love with him. Why, is another question of course, and may have bearing (may well), but I haven't enough data to go into that yet. G.H.C. would probably illustrate the falcon and its feeding-place, and that possibility must be borne in mind, but I'm rejecting it now (with reservations) on account of its slickness.

Don't like it. Don't like any of it. Rationalisation not unlike R.G.B.'s. Although I don't accept his details, I am neverthe-less almost sure that he suppressed certain facts, and that these facts may be more damning (in his view) than any of the others. I don't like any of this.

Point recurs *ad infinitum*. Is this a case for me?

February 15. Decided today after much thought to dis-continue Samson's verbatim notes in Jill's case. Decided also that it would not be advisable to discontinue notes with any of my other patients. This probably seems odd to Samson, but I see no need to explain it to her. Whole point is, verbatim notes have been helping me with the other patients and have perhaps been hindering with Jill. Left word on Samson's pad at lunch-time, but find now that she did not see instructions until after the session and accordingly took notes as usual. I did not know this, however, and observed marked improvement in results. Confident that my reception personality was better and that this was a factor in improvement. Got some good stuff, and feel that I am beginning to see my way through the maze. Still no sign of beginning of transference, however.

February 18. Took L. to the ballet last night. *Concurrence.* A great fuss about nothing. Why can't they find stories to tell?

February 21. A full day and a good day. Satisfactory results with J. F., followed by a good session with V., who has made a remarkable recovery and is now almost emancipated from me. And I have another aristocratic patient. The young Lord B. Bordering on idiocy, and probably not much I can do for him, but for all that I'm glad of him. It was Prof. S. who rang to tell me. "Know this is liable to be a bit of a bind for you," he said. "But remember the advertisement is good, and not only for you, but for analysis generally." Damnable really, I suppose, that one has to waste time dressing the window like this. Would be different in London. I think there one could afford to reject such cases, whereas here, as in all provincial towns, there is so much opposition and prejudice that one actually values an m.d. lord more than a genuine psychosis.

February 25. Worried Jill. Still no transference.

REVIEW.—Facts only. Include heresay facts, but no surmises or deductions.

Jill Waring, 21, only child, born mother's thirty-eighth year.

Family History.—No medical evidence of nervous or mental disease, although grandfather, founder of the shipping line and of Waring fortune, regarded as a character, and said to be "eccentric" (that damnable word that conceals so much from us in nine family histories out of ten). Grandfather stated by family to be "full-blooded man." Married life unhappy. Died 1930, cerebral thrombosis (arteriosclerosis). Parents unremarkable. Father constipated, inclined to meanness. A "good man." Told Jill repeatedly his ambition to double grandfather's fortune and die a millionaire. Died 1937, angina pectoris. Mother died 1943, empyema following pneumonia.

Patient's History.—Teething fits, said by Hughes-Brown to be "of no consequence." Walked 11 months. Talked (in phrases) 21 months. One "hysterical nurse" dismissed after about six months. Patient recalls very little about nurses, but volunteers that "one had a tooth which jumped." Patient said to have been very attached to grandfather, but does not remember him. He died when she was 2 years old. Was holding her on one occasion (age about 10 months) when he had a "shock" and dropped her. She was unhurt. Has no recollection, but, rationalising during free association, advances this as explanation of her repeated falling dreams.

All the usual childhood illnesses, plus scarlet. Normal course and convalescence.

Privately educated by governess from age 3 to 12. Governess still in family. "Very nice person. She spoiled me thoroughly and still does." Recollection of these years subnormal.

Started dancing lessons age 5, ballet lessons 7. M. commenced age 13.

School, Harrogate, 12-14. Unhappy. "I didn't get enough dancing." Scholastic standard—middle of class. V.G. music, but, note, backward maths. Formed strong attachment to housemistress, "who did not like me." Numerous references in free association to incident in second term, when parcel of sweets (which ought to have been handed in to housemistress for general distribution) discovered in patient's locker. Punishment severe lecture, including words "lying," "equivalent to stealing," "lack of moral sense" made considerable impression on patient. Wept for two days and refused food. Week in san. Was "never happy at school again, except sometimes when I was out with Jock" (pony at riding school). Removed from school at end of following year on advice of headmistress who wrote, "I am recommending this course only because I am satisfied that Jill has made up her mind not in any circumstances to allow herself to be happy with us here." (Patient not prepared to consent to my consulting head or housemistress.)

Educated by governess till age 17 and concurrently in dancing by pupil of Fokine (female). Rejected by R.A. of Dancing after examination. (This fact elicited with difficulty.)

Sent to finishing school, Lucerne. Fugue of two days' duration. Found in hotel in Lugano. Declared at the time she had no knowledge of how she got there, but says now merely covering up deliberate escapade with young American student of painting. (This explanation of doubtful reliability.) Brought home by air by family solicitor. Unsettled at home. Sent Paris study dancing. "Extremely happy." Beginning of association with Ballet Faméchon-Lisle. Morbidly interested in ballet, at this time to the exclusion of all else. (Talk still studded with refs. to ballet personalities, terms and history.)

August of last year patient learned that family solicitors are subsidising Ballet Faméchon-Lisle to the extent of £200 per annum. Greatly shocked. Troubled with the thought that it may only be because of the money that she has been accepted as member of the *corps de ballet*. Strong resistance here, and I have not had the full story. Same month, August, met R.G.B. Immediate attraction and of great intensity. (Adolescent hetero-sex experience negligible save for—unreliable—American painting student. Patient stresses her own frigidity, prior to meeting R.G.B.)

Summary of Emotional Attachments

1. Grandfather (pre-memory).

2. Father. "Very fond of Daddy. I always trusted him, though I don't think I really respected him."

3. Mother. "Was fond of her of course, but I liked Daddy best."

4. "Hammy" (Miss Hamilton, governess). "Hammy's a darling."

5. Housemistress. "I was terribly gone on her."

6. Mlle. Sauriac (dancing mistress). "I admired her the way you admire a character in a book. I kept trying, but I could never get through to her."

7. R.G.B. "Very much in love with him," but has a horror of bearing him children, "in case they should not be normal."

Symptoms.—Aural hallucinations of distant bells. Sees slight movements, as if of mice, at right angles to her eyes and just beyond her field of vision. (Her own description.) The bells invariably at night, the "mice" any time, but mostly twilight. Has full insight in these respects. Persistent sleeplessness and parieto-occipital headaches. Vivid dreams (texts of which I have noted elsewhere), and a degree of uncertainty as to whether she has actually undergone or dreamed certain experiences. A strong inclination, to which she has not yielded, to tell senseless lies. And—chief of all—the erotic phenomena of which R.G.B. has told me.

February 28. R.G.B. is impossible. On the doorstep this morning. Has been going over Grandfather Waring's papers and diaries on behalf of the family with a view to their publication next year in connection with some jubilee celebrations of the founding of the Waring line (75th anniversary, I think), and is now convinced that the whole key to Jill's troubles is to be found in the grandfather. Claims to have discovered real evidence of mental instability in the old man, and thinks this is vital information for me to have. "As far as I can make out," R.G.B. says, "he was more of the manic depressive type than the schizo" (!). Has left me a bundle of papers, and is determined that I should read them.

Am beginning to work up something of an anxiety neurosis myself on the Waring case. Took L. to the ballet again last night, and, coming away, commented, as I have done each time, on the ballerina. L. said, "Relax, darling. I'm getting tired of that red herring. I know quite well it's the outside left with the big mouth we go to see." I don't think Jill has a big mouth. Not noticeably big, anyhow. That's the make-up. But it's L.'s perception that startled me. I had thought that I had this interest, which is of course professional only, tucked well out of sight, and it is disturbing to learn that I am so tranparent.

On top of that another couple of incidents.

My mother and old Lady Greenskyres, both up in town oddly enough to try to get cooks, called after lunch, Mother wanting advice on a new issue of debenture stock, about which as usual I knew nothing, but I rang J.B., and he said buy. Both staying the night, and asked what show I recommended. I said, "Ballet," and realised with irritation that it was an automatic response. Mother said she thought she was too old for the ballet nowadays, and Lady G. said, "I'm not too old, but my husband is."

"But George isn't with you," Mother said.

"I know, dear," Lady G. said. "What I mean is, that George is too old for me to go to the ballet." Neat.

"That's too subtle for me, dear," my mother said. And it was of course. Old Lady G.'s double-entendres have yet to penetrate M.'s consciousness. Their friendship is the most incongruous and amusing I know.

But about the ballet. That *bon mot* of Lady G.'s has stuck in my mind all day, underlining what I have gradually been becoming aware of: that the ballet presents a tremendous field (virgin ground, too, far as I know) for the psychologist.

Audience, e.g. Why do people go to the ballet? What degree of identification? Psyche *v.* soma, to what extent can one separate the wolves from the sheep? And the ballet people themselves, a society within a society, utterly divorced from reality, inevitably narcissistic and erotogenic, their art a religion and their rites fetishistic, etc. God save me from a choreographer in my consultation room. Phew! Imagine the mental constellations! And how, supposing one is treating, to bring reality (our reality) to a patient who has spent most of his life at the barre, leg up, leg down, fouetté, pirouette and all the rest? How can such a patient ever have insight in the accepted sense? Is the ballet dancer, like the Mohammedan, beyond the Christian or Western psychologist? Is he merely game for the ætiologist? There is undoubtedly a paper here.

Psychology and the Ballet. Might have a stab at it some day. Meantime Jill. I have been coming to the conclusion in the last few days that preoccupation with ballet life is the determining factor in Jill's neurosis and that I have not probed this sufficiently. Wrote off a couple of days ago to Foyle's to send me everything they had on the ballet.

Fraser to see me. Jill leaving just as F. arriving and I had to introduce them. F. as always, genial and overpowering. Plainly impressed with Jill, and commented slyly afterwards on her looks and on my good fortune. Considered his remarks in bad taste and told him so. Seems now with unnecessary heat, as I know and knew that F. can't see a pretty girl without exercising this so-called humour of his. "My dear boy," F. said, "can't you take a joke? I'm not casting reflections on your professional conduct. Everybody knows you have a sense of honour the size of a hippopotamus, and if any of us had to send our wives to anybody, I assure you we'd send them to you." This is all very well, but it makes me out to be a bit of a stuffed shirt.

All right, suppose I am? . . . Fraser tells me J. is to do a pre-frontal leucotomy 11 a.m. tomorrow on the involutional melancholic whom he (F.) invited me to look at last week.

Books from Foyle's. A formidable pile. Examining them when Samson came in with a message from L. Wants me to ring her at six. Samson's lips curling at the books. "You are becoming quite a balletomane, Doctor."

"Miss Samson," I said, "you can go and get stuffed."

Never spoke to a woman in such a way in my life. Explanation presumably that I was smarting under Fraser's innuendoes (note even word association), and irritated because I know damned well that F. will read more into my reaction than justifiable. Thought about Samson repeatedly this afternoon and wondered if I should apologise or not. Even wondered if she might give notice, but meeting her on the stairs got a v. nice smile. "And you call yourself a psychologist!" as L. is always saying to me. Not quite the same, however, for with L. I'm on to every trick and deliberately pander to her illusions of superior feminine astuteness. Much relieved that Samson is not offended. Samson indispensable.

March 3. No session with Jill today. Went instead to afternoon tea at her home. This may not have been wise, but arranged the visit after careful consideration. Mainly to meet Aunt Bathia, but partly also out of curiosity of home circs. House big as a barracks and full of museum pieces, mostly the old grand-father's and retained by the aunt, another "character" (senile dementia), very much the grande dame, nineteenth-century dress, archaic speech, including much sailing-ship terminology, wig askew, totally bald (alopecia areata?). Extremely gracious, gave me the family history from Adam and wealth of useless information about Joshua (Capt. Waring: Jill's grandfather). Appeared unable to accept fact that I am a doctor and advised me repeatedly, "If you are seeking your fortune, young man, the best advice I can give you is to go to sea."

Jill very charming and normal. Tactful and gentle with aunt. Beauty of her movements particularly noticeable today. Wearing black woollen dress and pearls, self-colour nylons, and higher heels than usual. Observed bruise on left calf. Glancing from Aunt to Jill and sharing sympathetic insight, felt it incredible that this lovely girl should be a patient of mine.

R.G.B. knew about tea engagement and intended to be there, but did not turn up. Nearly ran him down at foot of the drive. Extremely anxious to have my reactions.

"Bit of a mausoleum, isn't it?" And when I said it was. "Did she show you her room?" (meaning Jill).

I said of course not and asked why, and he said, "Well, it's one of the things she does. Are you sure she didn't take you upstairs?" I snapped, and he changed the subject quickly, asking me if I had seen the library and expressing disappointment when I said I hadn't. He wanted to show me the papers he was working on and, in particular, the portrait by Holl of Joshua Waring. Told me he felt himself on the verge of a major psychological discovery. Already has the theory, and all he needs is the proof. R.G.B. is a crashing bore. I said that I thought he was overdoing the research, and suggested that he ought to leave it alone for a bit, but he assured me that he had never in his life come across anything so interesting, and would have dragged me back to the house to see his confounded papers if I had not pleaded an engagement and let in the clutch.

March 11. Well, R.G.B. has found his proof. Thing's too absurd to take seriously. However, for what it's worth, this is R.G.B.'s story.

The Waring fortune was built on murder. The murder was

committed by Joshua Waring (Jill's grandfather) who, as the young mate of a whaling ship, tipped his captain overboard on a stormy night, took over the captaincy of the ship, and from this choice beginning built up the fleet of ships (originally all whalers) which now fly the Waring flag. R.G.B. claims to have found indisputable proof of this in a secret diary, and says that the family solicitors have also in their possession a signed, sealed confession; and this of course is all quite probable. The gimmick is that R.G.B. has what he calls a parallel theory.

According to this v. ingenious theory the events of the past are about to repeat themselves, with Jill cast in the rôle of Joshua Waring, and the ballerina girl, Marie something, as the murdered captain. Other individuals, including myself, apparently fit into the piece too, and are identifiable, according to R.G.B., with persons of Joshua Waring's acquaintance immediately before the murder (e.g. Joshua was consulting a doctor at regular intervals to be leeched for blood impurities). R.G.B. convinced that the girl Marie is standing in Jill's way just as his captain stood in Joshua Waring's way, and that there is real danger that Jill will shortly hit on the same solution as her grandfather did.

I pooh-poohed the whole thing, of course, and explained at length that this so-called parallel theory wasn't psychologically sound, but couldn't shake R.G.B.'s conviction.

"It's possible though, isn't it?" he persisted.

I couldn't say that it wasn't, but assured him emphatically that in all the annals of practical psychology there was no recorded case of this type of parallelism.

"It could happen, though," R.G.B. argued.

I suppose it is the sort of thing that could happen once in a blue moon, but if it did it wouldn't have anything to do with psychology. It would be pure coincidence. R.G.B. so insistent that I had to get pretty sharp with him, and as a result he went off in a pet. The whole theory is utterly fantastic, but not untypical of the sort of thing one comes across with laymen psychologists. Mentioned it to Prof. S. at the club after dinner, without names, but got no response. "Make a nice bit of fiction," he said, and began to tell me an anecdote of the Mayo Clinic which he has told me at least twice already. Old boy's ageing.

March 13. Didn't sleep well last night, and found myself seriously considering R.G.B.'s nonsense. I have noticed of course that Jill feels an antagonism towards the ballerina girl, but have not considered this excessive or of particular significance. Question is, is this one of her resistances? Is she letting me get at the truth? Although R.G.B.'s theory is moonshine, it may contain a grain of sense, and that grain of sense (Jill's jealousy of the ballerina) may be one of the keys to the whole neurosis.

March 14. Jill in trousers today. "Hope you don't mind. It was Dickie's idea."

"Of course I don't mind," I said. "Why should I?"

"Well, you can't see my legs now," she said. "But as long as you don't mind."

Checked myself on the point of getting involved in this discussion on her legs and said briskly, "All right, let's get down to work, shall we?"

"It's just that I thought I'd seen you admiring my legs," she said maliciously.

"Stuff and nonsense," I said. But I was relieved that Samson had not heard that conversation.

The trousers didn't help. We had a full hour and got nowhere. Am getting increasingly worried about Jill. . . .

Rang up C.J. later in the afternoon and, finding him free,

went round to see him. Put the whole case to him. Told him my misgivings frankly, or at least frankly enough for him to read between the lines. I knew C.J. had it all by the time I finished.

"So what do you think?" I said. "Should I give it up?"

C.J. puffed his pipe and stared into the fire.

"I don't know, Johnny," he said. "Sort of thing you have to decide for yourself."

"But don't you see," I said, arguing against myself, "it's an odds-on chance that with an older man she would be willing to give far more that she's giving me?"

"Some of the older men," C.J. said, and did not complete his sentence.

"I know," I said, "I know. Some of them are impossible. But of course, I'd see she went to the right man. Phillips, for instance. The question is, having gone so far, should I hand over now?"

"It's up to you, Johnny."

"But what do you think? Honestly, C.J. You think that I ought to give it up, don't you?"

"Yes," C.J. said.

Definite enough, for all C.J.'s reluctance to say it, and I agree with him.

March 15. Rang L. after leaving C.J. last night and arranged to meet for dinner. Afterwards a gay evening and a hectic night. Imagine Fraser would not think me quite such a stuffed shirt if he could have spent last night with me. Thick head this morning and the beginnings of a cold. Have decided to persevere with Jill for one more week. I think that's fair enough. If at the end of that time I'm no forrarder, I'll pack in.

March 16. A better day. Realise I must have been out of sorts for the past few weeks. Took a small dose of soneryl last night and woke much refreshed. Saw V. at 11 a.m., and told him I thought he could now discontinue his visits, as his emancipation is complete. Sorry to lose him, for I think he is probably the most intelligent patient I have ever had and his insight all along has been such that I've learned a great deal from him. As for Jill—I'm convinced there is no significance in what little jealousy she feels for the ballerina girl. Thing's plain enough, and is admitted as a dislike on the conscious level. Below that there doesn't seem to be anything. Have probed it hard for the last three days, and am now satisfied that this is just one more red herring. Point to bear in mind—and I had lost sight of this—is that although my results to date with Jill are negative, they are, none the less, results. I *am* eliminating possibilities, and it might take another man weeks to cover this ground. Despite C.J.'s opinion, I don't think I would now be justified in giving up the case.

8.38 *p.m.*—This is fantastic. Someone has just tried to kill me. No possibility of a mistake. It's only by the grace of God that I'm still alive.

Had a late appointment (7 p.m.) with a man who couldn't come earlier, a greengrocer (suspect paraphrenia), first consultation. Sent Samson home. Showed my patient out at 8. Let myself out at about 8.25. Pitch dark. Opened my coat and put my key in my waistcoat pocket. Became aware suddenly of someone standing close to me, half turned, and as I did so, hand still in pocket, was violently forced back and thrown over the railings.

Ought to have fallen on my head on to the basement paving thirty feet below, but by sheer chance my left foot, kicking out, got caught in an open design at the foot of the railing, and I found myself hanging upside down, suspended by my foot. Quite unhurt save for a stinging pain in my ankle and a nasty bruise on the back of my head where I had struck against the stair-wall. Too surprised to call out or make any sound whatsoever. Hung there for several seconds, and heard my assailant walk slowly down the steps. Waited till footsteps had died away and then shouted. No one about, however. Managed to get my finger-tips on to a window-ledge below, and, having then taken some of the weight off my foot, was able to arrange it more comfortably and also to wedge the other foot into the railing. Then with much difficulty contrived to draw myself hand over hand up my own legs till I could get a grip on the railings. Let myself into the office again, locked the door, bolted the windows, put on all the lights, pulled down the blinds, and poured myself a very large one from the Distinguished Guest bottle.

Sat down and tried to think, but couldn't think, partly I suppose because of the pain in my head and partly because of the whisky. Surely couldn't have been the greengrocer? Had to tell somebody and rang C.J. C.J. out, so got Fraser, told him what had happened, and he said he'd come right round.

And there the thing rests. Who could possibly want to murder me, and for what conceivable reason? Just beginning to feel shaky, and think I'm entitled to another snort. . . .

Fraser hasn't come yet, but there's no longer any mystery. Telephone rang a few minutes ago. Sergeant at the Park Street Police Station. "Are you all right, sir?"

"Of course I'm all right," I said. "Why?"

"Well," the sergeant said, and I heard him smiling. "Fact is, there's a man here says he just murdered you. Says he threw you off the bridge of a ship."

"Who?" I shouted.

"Well, he says his name is Captain Joshua Waring, but he doesn't look like a seafaring man to me. Fact, if you ask me, he's M.D., sir."

"You're holding him?" I asked.

"Yes, of course."

"I'll be right over," I said.

But I think I'll wait for Fraser. I've got to think. I've got to work this out before I face R.G. It is R.G.B., of course. I think I knew all along that it was R.G.B. And I think I knew, too, or I certainly ought to have known, that something like this was liable to happen. Can't understand now how I could ever have let this come about. My God, the signs were all there, clear enough for a Boy Scout to read. And I missed every one of them. I've been so preoccupied with Jill that I never once turned the full glare of my mind on R.G.B. I knew he was the hysterical type, of course, and I knew he had a bee in his bonnet over Joshua Waring and this parallel nonsense—which was nonsense only when applied to Jill. Never occurred to me that the parallel theory might be a delusion—a clinical delusion—of R.G.B.'s—and a delusion of course which became so strong and obsessional that R.G.B. himself was forced into the position of J. Waring—it's so clear now that my neglect is incomprehensible, almost criminal. Legally, I'm all right at least. He wasn't my patient. I've no legal responsibility. But that doesn't alter the fact that I know I'm to blame.

Another aspect that I haven't even considered yet—the most important of all: Jill. This is tremendous. This completely alters the case, ends it, in fact. Jill isn't a case at all, never has been. God, I'm pleased! And all that stuff about her erotism, all that stuff that worried and puzzled me so much—how could I have missed seeing that that was a fiction—the clearest symptom of all of R.G.B.'s derangement! No use pretending that this doesn't mean a great deal to me. Opens up all sorts of possibilities that were out of the question before. But I must go slow. She'll be very distressed over R.G.B. That's the worry now. How she'll take it. No question that she was in love with him or fancied she was. And this is bound to be a great shock to her. I must be patient. I'll be patient, my darling. You'll never have known anyone so patient. Must stop writing or I'll make a B.F. of myself. Whisky's going to my head.

March 14. Fraser and I went round to the police station last night and examined R.G.B. There wasn't much to be done. R.G.B. in a dull confused state, although the sergeant said he had shown signs of violence earlier. Arranged for him to be admitted to the Gardner Institute, waited for the ambulance, and went along with him. R.G.B. then completely mute. Nothing I could do for him. Gave Simmonds an outline of the facts, and gladly accepted his offer of an ambulance to drive me home.

Rang up the theatre, but couldn't get Jill. After much hesitation telephoned the house and spoke to Aunt Bathia, obviously straight from bed, and using the telephone like a ship's megaphone. Broke the news as tactfully as I could. Aunt Bathia quite unperturbed. "Not at all surprised," she shouted. "And don't tell me that young man is ill. He's mad. Mad as a hatter. I always said so."

I liked that. Liked it enough to tell it to Prof. S. at lunch, and it was only when he was paying me my tribute in the form of that big belly laugh of his that I felt a flush of Escariotism. Whose lectures was it? . . . *"When you feel the pangs of remorse, and, gentlemen, you will, you can always assuage your guilty conscience by noting the matter with pious repentance in your private case books."* Fact remains, damned indiscreet of me.

Have been wondering all day how and when to get in touch

with Jill. Think it would be best to leave her completely alone for a few days, and then perhaps some flowers and a card, then call. Would like to ask C.J.'s advice, but daren't.

Had an appointment with Jill at 3 p.m., but in the circumstances did not expect her to keep it. After three when I returned from lunch. Samson very cool. "Miss Waring is waiting, Doctor."

Went into my room, suprarenal glands working to capacity. She was lying on the couch, the blind down as usual. I spoke sympathetically about R.G.B., and was very relieved to note that she appeared to be taking it in a normal sensible way. I said, to brighten her up, "I didn't expect you today, you know, and I doubt if there's any need for you to come again. There's really nothing much the matter with you."

"That's what I've been telling you for weeks," Jill said.

"I know," I said. "I'm sorry. I was quite misled. I had a lot of inaccurate information about you. . . ."

"From Dickie?"

"Yes."

"And you believed it?"

"Yes, I'm afraid I did." It seemed very ridiculous now, but I couldn't say so. There were innumerable things that I couldn't say, things I wanted very much to say and wouldn't be able to say for a long time yet. But I knew I'd say them some day, and I knew too that there was no hurry. I was very happy.

"Poor Dickie," Jill said. "I never would have come to you, you know, in the first place if it hadn't been for Dickie. He was determined to make a case out of me. But we won't speak about Dickie. Are you sure I'm all right now?"

"Pretty sure," I said. "The pieces of the jig-saw are beginning to fall into place, and I have to admit it's quite a relief. I was very puzzled over you for a while."

"Poor darling," she said. Yes, she said that! "Come and tell me about it," and she held out her hand to me. Saw her face clearly for a moment in a band of sunlight. Eyes indescribably beautiful. I sat down on the edge of the couch. I was sick with feeling for her, and I knew I would have to be very careful not to make a complete ass of myself. She said something softly, but I didn't hear. I had just noticed that her coat had fallen open, and that, apart from her shoes and stockings, she hadn't a stitch of clothing on.

And then, as I was ringing for Samson, she had to say that terrible, unforgettable thing, oh God, she said it in all sincerity. "I don't know how to thank you enough," she said, "for all you've done for me."

THREE FINGERS ARE PLENTY

WHEN I WAS A CHILD I WAS DOMINATED BY A BOY I SHALL call Kirk. I was brought up in a proud old town on the Moray Firth coast of Scotland, and I was brought up in the North Scottish Presbyterian way, that is, Very Properly Indeed. I have never really understood, therefore, why I was allowed to make a friend of Kirk, for Kirk was far from proper. He was a kind of Scotch Huckleberry Finn—a boy who went barefoot, wore orra patched breeks, smoked a clay cutty, chewed plug tobacco, jeuked the school. By all the standards of our time and place, Kirk was beyond the pale. He even worked on Sundays.

Kirk lived with Baggie McLaughlin and his hairy old wife in the cottage at the foot of our hill. Baggie was a small wizened man who touched his forelock to everyone, even me aged eight, and always walked on the grass verge of the road. He called himself a pig-sticker. He went round the outlying crofts at Martinmas, killing off the pigs at a shilling a time, and this was the only work he ever admitted to. In fact, he was a beachcomber. Kirk used sometimes to say that he was a retired pirate, but I knew quite well that this was an exaggeration. Baggie would not have said boo to a gosling.

His wife was very old. I suppose she must have been about the same age as Baggie, but she looked much older. She was crippled with arthritis, bent like a right angle, and heavily bearded. She rose late and retired early, and when she wanted to go to bed she would hobble to the cottage door and ring a big ship's bell that Baggie had picked off the shore, and then Kirk had to run home and help get her into bed. He said it was a hell of a job getting her into bed, and I bet it was, for she was solid as teak and must have weighed close on sixteen stone.

As far as anybody knew, Kirk had lived all his life with this old couple, but even I, who had no biological knowledge, knew that he did not belong to them. He was of different stock. He looked every man in the eye and touched his forelock to none. As I remember him he was tall for his age, straight as a mast, flat-backed, and uncommonly broad across the shoulders. His hair was red, and he wore it very long, except when Baggie put a bowl on top of it and cut round the rim, and then he was a sorry sight—but nobody ever laughed at him. At least, no boy did.

The most remarkable thing about him was his eyes. I never noticed the colour of anyone else's eyes until I grew up and started looking at girls, but I could not help noticing Kirk's. They were greenish-blue, the colour of blue-bottle flies in the sun, and they were full of devil. When Kirk flicked me with these blue-bottle eyes of his and said, "What are we waiting for?" I just automatically said, "Let's go." I always said it, and I always went. I guess I'd have gone anywhere at all with Kirk.

Kirk was a year and nine months older than me. When he was ten he built a boat out of three-ply wood and petrol-cans, and we sailed this boat on the open sea. We were often afloat for the whole day, and sometimes we went so far out to sea that we lost sight of land. When it blew up we shipped a lot of water, and then I baled like fury with two Rowntree cocoa tins while Kirk sat cross-legged in the stern, keeping her bows up to the seas by judicious management of his oar (my sister's tennis racket with the gut out and a sheet of tin nailed in its place). He was never at a loss, never rattled—never afraid—and twenty years ago I had much the same degree of confidence in Kirk and his three-ply *Ruler of the Waves* as I now have in Captain Illingworth and the *Queen Mary*.

One day, during an aquatic gala in the harbour of a small town nine or ten miles up the coast, Kirk paddled through the bottle-neck into the basin, and allowed himself to be captured by the judges' launch. When they asked where he had come from, he pointed out to sea and said, "Norge." The local folks made a great fuss of him, presented him to Lady somebody or other who was there for the prize-giving, fed him on chocolate and ice-cream, and billeted him with the Minister. The Minister had then three young daughters—one of whom is now my wife—and she has told me that Kirk made such a powerful impression, what with slapping his chest, emitting guttural growls, and declaiming "Ach so?" that she and her sisters were all slightly in love with him for weeks.

The imposture lasted less than a day, but it happened to be the day the weekly county paper went to press, and our normally reliable journal came out with a sober account of Kirk's adventure under the heading, "YOUNG VIKING'S EXPLOIT."

In due course Kirk and his boat were sent home in one of Alexander's big blue buses, the story was the talk of the town, and my father, discovering that I had sometimes gone to sea with Kirk, thrashed me judicially and, with an axe over his shoulder, marched me down to Baggie's cottage, where he fulminated against Kirk and duly despatched the boat. It is characteristic of Kirk that while my father was telling Baggie exactly what he meant to do to *that boy* if ever he laid hands on him, that boy was grinning smugly down at us from a branch not six feet above my father's head.

Kirk was always one jump ahead of the other fellow. I am sure that was the secret of his leadership. When a gang of us went guddling, Kirk would coax a whole frying of sizeable trout into his thick fingers while the rest of us puddled with a few miserable sticklebacks. If we went along the cliffs to rob gulls' nests, it was Kirk who spotted the best colonies and only Kirk who would dare climb to them. It was Kirk who first showed us a bowline on the bight and a Turk's head, who made fish-hooks for us out of horse-shoe nails, who taught us to lift and *cope* a ferret, who assembled the radio for our KU-KLUX clubroom. He was a born leader. He was always out in front, and whenever there was anything important to be done it was always Kirk who did it best.

.   .   .   .   .   .

The people of my home town still talk about Kirk's jumping.

The first time he jumped from the Brig o' Doom was one Sunday afternoon when he would have been about twelve. We had gone for a walk, the pair of us, and we were leaning over the parapet of the Brig looking for salmon swirls in the pool some sixty feet below when Kirk said, "Bet you couldn't jump it." I said, "Bet you couldn't either," and Kirk jumped it.

When I told them at school they wouldn't believe me, and I laid bets wholesale, and the following Saturday the whole school turned up to see Kirk jump from the Brig again. Everybody was scared stiff when he climbed up on the parapet, but after it was all over some of the older boys said it was easy enough that side, they'd like to see him do it on the other side, between the rocks, *that's* where they had bet he wouldn't jump. So Kirk jumped on the other side, between the rocks, and while he was jumping Alan Maxwell fainted, and at least half of us didn't dare look. Kirk said it was easy, he would jump it any time we wanted, but none of us who had seen him do it wanted to see him do it again. Of course there were some who had missed the fun, and so for several Saturdays Kirk, accompanied by bands of boys, went out to Doom, and for a collection of pennies, marbles, chewing-gum, etc., jumped from the Brig.

Next it was the Town Bridge. I don't know who first threw out the challenge by saying it was impossible to jump from the Town Bridge, it might have been any of us, for—goodness knows—we all knew very well how impossible it was. The Town Bridge is even higher than Doom, and there isn't more than five or six feet of water at the deepest point.

Kirk was to jump at ten o'clock on a Saturday morning, and by nine o'clock there was such a press of boys on the bridge that traffic was at a standstill, there were hooting lines of cars at both ends, and the police were out in force trying to move us on. When Kirk appeared, Sergeant Munro, I think it was, collared him and led him by the scruff of the neck to the police station. Kirk said he had a bad time in the police station, he didn't exactly get the third degree, but he had a thoroughly bad time; he was told all about Borstal, and he was told that he would be sent there, broken neck and all, if he ever dared jump from the Town Bridge. They kept him in the police station for over an hour, and when Kirk came out he said he would be there still if he hadn't finally promised, Scout's honour, that he wouldn't jump from the bridge.

Well, Kirk didn't jump.

He dived, and he got off lightly, breaking only his left arm and collar-bone and cracking open his skull across his two crowns.

He wasn't sent to Borstal, but he spent five weeks on his back in Palmer's Hospital.

.   .   .   .

When Kirk was thirteen Baggie said it was time he stopped scrimshanking and learned a trade. Actually Kirk had worked at odd jobs from the time he was able to walk—lifting potatoes, picking rasps, delivering papers and groceries, shovelling coke in the gasworks, helping mysteriously in the blacksmith's shop, and so on—but of course there wasn't any future in these jobs, and I suppose that Baggie was thinking only of what was best for Kirk when he decided to apprentice him to Old John Low, the tailor.

Kirk felt terrible about it. He said flatly that he wasn't going to be a tailor. He wasn't going to do woman's work in a stuffy shop, not him; he had set his heart on the sea, and he was going to sea and be damned to them all. There were some desperate scenes in the cottage at the foot of the hill, and after one of them, when Baggie had thrashed him with a strap, Kirk ran away. He was caught in Aberdeen on board an Icelandic trawler and sent home, and he spent exactly one day at work in the tailor's shop. On the evening of that day Baggie came up to our house and, with a great flurry of lock-touching, asked to see my father.

"It's aboot ma loon, Kirk," he said, panting.

"Fit's wrang wi' your loon?" our maid asked.

"Ma loon's took the chopper and chopped off his thimble finger," Baggie said.

My father listened in amazement to the story and gave his advice. His advice was to send the boy to sea, and the sooner the better.

Kirk was duly sent to sea and disappeared from my life. I wrote him twice, addressing my letters to the Assistant Cook aboard the trawler *Esmeralda*, c/o the Aberdeen Trawling Company, but I did not get any reply. I have not seen Kirk since that day nearly twenty years ago when he came to say good-bye with all his worldly possessions in a small sack on his back and his right hand still in bandages.

But although I have not seen him I have thought of him often. At moments of crisis my mind seems always to have returned to Kirk, and I am deeply conscious of having hitched my wagon to the stars which he, in childhood, showed me. It was Kirk who taught me by his example that a man must be true to himself, no matter what the cost, and that lesson has stood me in good stead at all the cross-roads in my life. It was because of Kirk's example that I dug my heels in and insisted that I was going to be a writer, not a doctor. It was because of Kirk that I dared to marry long before I could afford to. It was because of Kirk that, when war broke out, I chose to go to sea rather than join Naval Intelligence and sit in an office job ashore. And then, during the war, when things happened to me—when my ship was blown up under me in the North Sea, when I was attacked by a pack of U-boats on Atlantic convoy, and when I swept five mines in twenty minutes off Normandy on D-day minus one— it was mainly because I had moulded my life on Kirk that I was able to behave, in these testing moments, in a way that I like to think was adequate. Again and again I have found myself thinking of that red-headed boy, imagining him as a much-decorated fighter pilot, as a parachutist on a hopeless mission, as the leader of a suicidal guerrilla band, and whenever I have felt my spirits flag, when I have been faced with a problem that has seemed too big for me, I have summoned up a picture of Kirk and I have asked myself, "What would *he* do?" And of course the thing that Kirk would do has always been the thing which has been most difficult for me to do, but it has also been the right thing—and once in a while I've done it.

I owe Kirk a debt that I can never repay.

Although I have not seen him since we were boys together, I *have* heard of him. On Christmas Eve, 1945, when we were clearing the last of the Mediterranean minefields, a Sammy mine popped up underneath my ship and blew her stern off. We were towed into Algiers, and those officers who had lost their gear went ashore to find a tailor.

They found a very good one in a little shop off the *place du Gouvernement*, a genial and characterful Scotsman who had lost a finger fighting pirates in the China Seas. They were pleased with the gear he sold them, and they brought back his card and stuck it on the wardroom notice-board. Translated, it read:

KIRK McLAUGHLIN
European Tailor
75 rue Bab Azoun
Algiers

CLASSY CLOTHES FOR CLASSY GENTS

It was unmistakably Kirk.

PORTRAIT OF MANUEL

I ONCE PAINTED A PICTURE THAT I LIKED. REALLY LIKED. A picture that was great. It was a picture of a fairground on a rainy morning, and I painted it in Puente Genil, in Andalusia, the day after Manuel Garcio lost his pigtail and his life. I painted it in gaslight. It was raining that day, and I closed the shutters in my hotel room and painted all day and all night. The following morning the sun came out, and I mopped up the worst of the wet on the floor with a shirt, and I saw then that I had painted a picture that was great.

I do not like to describe paintings. There is no subtlety to words and no immediacy. You cannot ever tell anybody about a painting. You can tell that it is good or bad, and you can tell the subject-matter, and that is all. The subject of this painting was a fairground on a wet day. It was painted from memory. The fair was a familiar scene to me, because when Fern finally left her husband and children and came to me, we took a flat overlooking the fairground and lived there for the three months that we had together before they took Fern to the sanatorium.

I used to sit at the window looking down at the fair, and

Fern would come and put her arms round me, low down, and hold tight, her hair falling over my face. There was a great power in me then, and I remember saying to her, "Some day I'll make a job of this fair!" And there, in the expensive bughouse in Puente Genil I made the job, although I had not thought of the fair for many years, and did not know, when I sat down to work, that I was going to paint it. I can't tell you about it. It was the only thing I have ever done that satisfied me, and I am afraid that it may be the only thing that ever will. It was quite great.

When I had finished it I put it against the wall out of the sun, locked the door, told the Señora with the emphatic double negative that my room was not on any account to be entered, and went down the Aquilar Road to the house of Señor Priego, where I had taken Manuel's widow and three children the day before.

Señor Priego was the husband of Manuel's Aunt Ana. He lived in a house that had two stone shields of hidalgos on its peeling stucco front. He had lineage and had once had wealth. He was a small man, and he looked distinguished and inbred. He distrusted me because I was a foreigner, and yesterday, thinking of his prestige, he had been very angry with me for bringing the widow and the children. I never met the Señora, Manuel's aunt. I never succeeded in getting inside the house.

Señor Priego would not allow me to see Maria.

"The grief of the widow is inconsolable," he said. "I will bear your commiserations in person."

"But I must see her," I said. "I want to say good-bye. I am leaving this evening. I am returning to England."

"It is a source of considerable regret," Señor Priego said. "But the widow is prostrate, and it is not permitted to intrude upon such desolation."

He was adamant.

"It is much regretted," he said.

"All right, listen," I said. "Tell her I am going back to England, that I have a picture of great value; I intend to sell my picture, it will bring much money, a thousand *duros*, possibly more. Tell her that I will send the money to her. Is it clearly understood?"

"It is clearly understood. It will be of interest."

"It is well, then," I said. "God be with her, and this house."

When I crossed the patio a voice called, "Ingleez!" and, looking up, I saw Manuel's eldest son, Ramon, aged seven, waving to me from the *azotea*.

"Ingleez," he called. "The death of my father was creditable, is it so?"

"It is so, Ramon," I said. My vision blurred when I looked at him, and I turned away. "*Adios*."

"*Adios* also to you," Ramon said. "I knew always that it was creditable to a high degree. I shall make a manifestation of it to my uncle."

I walked back along the Aquilar Road to my hotel. The sun was getting hot. There was a heat-mist shimmering in the hills at the back of the town and a glitter on the white road. One of the beggars selling birds stopped me, holding the three-inch cage up to my eyes.

"Is the bird blind?" I asked.

It was a green singing finch.

"*Si*, Señor. *Si, si*."

"In that case I shall not have it," I said, leaving him to gape after me. It must surely be known even to the mad English that one always blinded the birds!

At my hotel they told me that the police had called again. They had expressed great interest in the fact that my room was locked and had required to be shown the door, but they had made no attempt to force it.

"Ah, this matter of politics !" the Señora said, hands high. "The tragedy it is !"

"There is no cause for anxiety," I assured her. "I go today. I leave by the afternoon train."

"I made it clear to them," she said. "They are content."

"It is well. I donate my lottery ticket to you, Señora."

"A thousand thanks, Señor."

I went up to my room. Someone had entered in my absence and all my belongings had been handled. The painting was intact. I sat on the bed and examined it. I did not quite believe that it was my own work. It was too good. It was life in the rain. It was flamboyant and brave and sad and beautiful. It was truly great. I took up a brush and wrote in a corner, "Portrait of Manuel." I kept the writing small.

2

I met Manuel Garcio in Madrid during what must have been, I suppose, the most difficult period of his life. It was the summer of 1937, the siege of Madrid had just begun, and Manuel was making arrangements to evacuate his family and himself to Catalonia, where his manager had a farm.

I was in Madrid simply because I had been there at the outbreak of war and because I had no particular reason to go home; and also because I was curious. God help me, I thought it would divert me to watch a war.

I met Manuel in the Bar Atocha on the Callé, the hill that leads from the working-class district to that Piccadilly of Madrid, the Puerta del Sol. I had noticed him several times before I learned who he was. He sat alone. Even when the bar was packed, his privacy was not disturbed. There were always vacant seats at his table. He sat stiff-backed, and in this city of proud men he was conspicuously proud and aloof. I became aware that although no one spoke to him, everyone was conscious of him, and one day, studying his neat *coleta* or pigtail, I said to my friend Esteban Maltés, the wine merchant: "He is a bull-fighter, is he not?"

"He is a great bull-fighter. He is Manuel Garcio."

I looked at Manuel with new interest.

"If he had fought this season he would have equalled Belmonte in the number of his bulls, and there are those who declare him to have greatness exceeding Belmonte's because he imposes no conditions and does not select his bulls."

"Do you know him?" I asked.

"I knew him," Esteban said.

"I don't understand. You mean, he's on the other side?"

"He is on neither side."

I was intrigued.

"Will you introduce me?"

"No," Esteban said. "You will find no one to introduce you."

It was true.

"That poltron," they said. "That craven. That artist. I spit in his eye. I defile the bones of his mother, yea, gladly." No one had a good word for Manuel Garcio, and no one would introduce me.

Finally, one evening I went to his table.

"Is it permitted that I sit here?" I asked.

He looked at me gravely.

"I would esteem it a privilege to sit with you, Señor."

"It is permitted," he said.

We did not talk much that first night. He would have none

of my *fundador* or cigarettes. He smoked a black foul cigar, and drank only a red wine that I later tasted and found almost non-alcoholic.

"I understand you are not running the bulls this season," I said.

"No."

"But you will run the bulls again, undoubtedly?"

"After the war, Señor, undoubtedly."

"When do you think the war will end? The Insurgents make progress, do they not?"

"They capture terrain, admittedly."

"Do you think they will win?"

"I have not a knowledge of such affairs."

I liked him despite his taciturnity, and I was sorry for him. It became the custom for me to sit at his table each evening, and when he saw clearly that I too was a neutral and an artist, his suspicions relaxed and he was glad of my company.

One evening Esteban Maltés came in and stood in the door-way searching for an acquaintance.

"There is your friend," Manuel said, his voice tinged with bitterness.

"Señor," I said, "I am sitting with my friend."

It was from that date, I think, that our friendship really began.

I learned that his arrangements to leave Madrid were almost complete. He had negotiated the lease of his house, and was waiting only for the sale of his household effects arranged for the end of the month. He was quite determined to leave Madrid, yet derived no pleasure from the prospect. He appeared to be completely honest and insufferably vain.

"Consider," he said. "If I fight in the war, whether for the Republic or the Falange, I am in an army, I am one of many, and with no distinction. Neither my commander nor the flying lead of the enemy knows me, that I am Manuel Garcio, the *torrero*. I am a soldier, simply. It would be of an unspeakable stupidity for Manuel Garcio to risk his life in this fashion, for Manuel Garcio and his art belong to the whole nation, verily, neither to this faction nor that, and the nameless death of a soldier would be a degradation to me and to Spain, equally. Is it clear to you also, that are an artist?"

"Yes and no, Manuel," I would say. I was familiar with both sides of this Ivory Tower argument, but I was not accustomed to hear the artist assess his own worth so high and so frankly. "For instance, is it not possible that an artist, who necessarily is also a man, may be answerable first to his soul and only in the second place to his artistic conscience?"

"It is not possible, *amigo*. Consider me the man. I am of no worth. I am a shepherd or a butcher or a wine vendor. I am nothing."

"You are a man," I said. "It is enough. Consider your individuality in this respect. Consider your distinguishing pride. Consider your position in the family that you love."

"The butcher also has a wife of much charm and affection, and the shepherd also is master in his house."

"Is it not then," I persisted, "the duty of the *torrero* of great fame to set an example of courage to the people, to lead the people?"

"The rebels have El Caudillo and there are many commanders in the Government. It is the duty of the great *torrero* to act with dignity everlastingly and to preserve himself for Spain."

"It is hard to combine these duties."

"It is possible."

Oddly enough, I once saw Manuel combine dignity with self-preservation. It was the evening that the attempt was made to wipe out the Puerta del Sol, block by block. We heard the first wave of planes coming over very low and everyone in the bar went for cover—under the bar itself, the tables, the benches. That is, everyone except Manuel. Manuel marched out of the door. When there was a lull in the explosions we all resumed our seats, and in a few minutes Manuel entered, as dapper and disdainful as ever.

"Where did you go?" I asked.

"I went to the lavatory."

"The lavatory!"

"To lie down in public is not conceivable to me," Manuel said.

I looked at him closely. He was perfectly serious.

3

Manuel left Madrid. I stayed on. I did not see him again for eighteen months, during which time I got mixed up in this war and, to my surprise, became a soldier, although not a very useful one. I finally left Madrid in March 1939, when our side split into two groups and we got orders to eliminate those of our comrades who, under the extremist Colonels, Barcelo and Bueno, wished to fight Franco to the end. There was no longer any sense in anything. Our leaders had got to the stage of using honeyed words. They were selling us, and we all knew it. We knew that in a day or two Franco's red and gold banners would fly over Madrid, and on the night of March the sixth bands of us, who wanted neither to kiss the Moors' backsides nor slaughter the men who had fought as our brothers, left the city to its new, bloody civil war, and deserted.

I heard quite by accident that Manuel Garcio was in Cordoba. I was making by easy stages for Algeciras, which is only a stone's-throw from Gib., and I was in a café in a little town called Los something, on the southern bank of the Guadalamez, when I heard a party of Falangists mention the name of Manuel Garcio. Listening, I learned that Manuel was in Cordoba and that he was just as unpopular with the Falangists as he had been with the Loyalists in Madrid. I had little sympathy to spare for Manuel's plight, however. My money was almost at an end, and I was desperate.

It was only afterwards, thinking of Manuel's pleasure at seeing me, that I realised how lonely he must have been and how deeply he was hurt by the attitude of his countrymen who suffered him only for his past glory and considered him now beneath contempt.

Manuel and his wife and three children were living in a large stucco apartment house on the north side of the city. He kept pumping my hand and smiling. I do not remember ever having seen him smile in Madrid. His wife, who had been very pretty but, still young, was thickening in the Spanish manner, was happy to see me too, for Manuel's sake. After a meal and a series of extravagantly phrased, non-political toasts, Manuel said: "You will remain in my house under my protection. I shall arrange it."

"Do you think you can?" I said dubiously. "Have you enough influence?"

"Señor!"

"All right, big shot," I said in English, grinning. He went off that same evening—I understood from Maria, who lost colour and did not regain it until he returned, that he had gone to see the Mayor—and came back after midnight to say that it was arranged, I was to enjoy the amenities of the city as his guest. I never knew how he had arranged it, and I did not question him. He would not have liked it. I saw that it gave him great pleasure to show me in this casual fashion that he still had influence.

In the fortnight that I lived with Manuel and his family it became clear to everyone that the war was ended. Peace negotiations were openly conducted by radio. A Government delegation flew to Burgos for a conference with Franco. While the term unconditional surrender stuck in the governmental gullet, Franco sent troops against the Cordoba front and the Loyalists surrendered everywhere. On the morning of Tuesday the 28th of March, Madrid fell. The Spanish Civil War was over.

There was great jubilation among the Insurgents, now the masters of Spain, and everywhere, even in the Loyalist districts, flags appeared in the streets, pipe bands played, and every day was a fiesta or public holiday.

On the 1st of April the police came to Manuel's house. We were all in the patio, and Ana Franca, aged four, was sitting on my knee reciting nursery rhymes to me with her mouth full of orange.

"Hush, Ana," her mother said.

Ana did not hush. It was difficult for me to hear what the Chief of Police said. I made out that he had come to bestow a signal honour on Señor Manuel Garcio, who was required on the fifth day of the month to run the bulls at Granada by order of, in honour of, and in the very presence of, an Important Personage. He trumpeted the name.

"It is indeed an honour," Manuel said. "Yet I decline."

"You do not understand, Señor. This is a privilege of the highest degree that has been accorded you. It is also an order."

"I decline."

"Manuel!" his wife said.

"It is emphasised that it is the wish of the General that Señor Manuel Garcio should lend his presence to the *Corrida de Toros*."

"It is indeed an honour, but I decline. It must be permitted that I myself make a selection of the dates on which I run the bulls, naturally."

"Señor!" the Chief of Police said. He was very angry. He was red in the face and his chest was swollen. He towered above Manuel. Manuel's head was on a level with the Chief of Police's shoulder, and there was an implacable purpose in his eyes.

"Señor, you will run the bulls. Is it clearly understood?"

"No," Manuel said. "I am in opposition. I regret it."

The child had stopped talking.

"Manuel, oh, Manuel!" Maria said.

He glanced sharply at her and she turned away, colouring, but almost immediately looked back at him, the same shameless expression of love in her face. "Manuel, please!" she said.

He stared at her for what seemed a very long time. I had stopped breathing. Gradually the rigidity went out of his shoulders and his eyes became gentle.

"Then let it be thus," he said.

4

Today there are many people who believe that Manuel Garcio was a Communist. This is not true. He was no more a Communist than I am. He was of importance—the phrase is his own—and the cipher status of man would have been equally intolerable to him under any totalitarian regime. He belonged to no party. He was, quite simply, an individualist.

He was a Spaniard, and his own man. He certainly was not a Communist; and as a matter of fact the only political remark I can recall hearing him make was one in praise of the Falange.

"Under the new regime," he said, "there is a great efficiency in arrangement."

We were then in Granada, Manuel and Maria and the three children and myself, and we were sitting at one of the white wicker tables in the Arcade looking down on the procession that marked the opening of the fiesta.

"There is certainly a great efficiency," he said.

It was true. We had been brought from Cordoba to Granada with an efficiency which, in Spain, was frightening. The police car that took us to the station had arrived at the prearranged time. We found our seats in the train reserved, and at Granada a car was waiting to drive us to the Metropole, an oasis of palms and chipped spittoons where we were formally welcomed and shown to the rooms that the authorities had booked for Señor Garcio and party.

"There is even an efficiency in the waiters," Manuel said. "Boy, more cognac!"

"Before, he has never moistened his lips prior to a *Corrida*," Maria said to me, casting an anxious glance at Manuel. "Never, I inform you. Not by the kiss of a cork."

"It is an occasion. Before there has never been a liberation," Manuel said. "And I call you to observe it, woman. This is but my second."

"More *jerez* for Maria," I said.

"*Nada*," Maria said. "Nothing more."

The procession rounded the town buildings and was now in the flagged square below us, the band leading, the reeds very shrill, the drums hollow. A standard bearer marched in front of the band, and by his side a sandwichman bearing a large photograph of El Caudillo before and behind him. Children with balloons danced round them. Then came a token platoon of Franco's Moors, with bayonets fixed, all spit and polish; and behind the Moors, quite dwarfed, marched the religious and civic dignitaries. Behind came the dancers, their white-putteed legs twinkling, and interspersed among them were monster figures of fable and local history. A man in a blue suit walked in their midst wheeling a barrow full of rockets, one of which he ignited every few minutes. The procession dwindled away into a straggling mass of townspeople in holiday dress, waving flags and bearing banners on long poles, all laughing and singing. There were families on all the balconies and flat-topped *azoteas*. They threw flowers and bright streamers, and called to the people they knew, or if they knew no one they just called: "*Viva!*"

After the procession had marched three times round the Square, it began to disappear through the miniature arch of Carlos the Third which led to the stadium, and then we watched the people who followed the procession. These people were not strictly part of the procession. They were mostly country families who had come into town for the fiesta, and they were determined to miss nothing. They pressed in a tight swarm through the streets. Here and there a man played on a reed pipe and women beat on their fibre baskets. Some of the men wore brown baggy corduroys and most of the women had shawls. The children were bare-footed, and all—men, women, children—carried enough food and wine to last a fortnight. Some led *burros* and some had brought their mules, which they drove with sharp, pointed sticks. They kept shouting to each other and to their animals. They gesticulated at the rockets and at the balconies. They made loud jokes. They were all deliriously happy. It was the fiesta. *Viva, viva!* The war was ended!

I remembered many things, and I felt a momentary bitterness at this fiesta and at Manuel sitting by my side drinking cognac with such a bored expression, as aloof and detached from the celebrations as he had been from the war itself. It did not seem right that any man should be so indifferent to the common emotions of his countrymen.

"I have an aunt who lives near," Manuel said to me. "At Puente Genil. She is married to a man of some nobility and they have a great affection for my Maria."

"Do you expect, then, to see them?"

"No," Manuel said. "I merely tell you."

"We must eat," Maria said. "Manuel, you will wish to see the bulls, and you must go early so that they can dress you with a complete perfection."

"I have no desire to see the bulls," Manuel said. "But we will eat."

5

They had given us a box beside the President's. The President's box was empty save for the President himself, and the boxes on both sides of the President's box were empty. Every other seat was occupied. Although the heat of the sun was intense, there was not even a single space in the hard stone *tendinos* on the *Sol*. The empty boxes were reserved for the General.

Two bulls had already been despatched before the Great Man arrived. When the President heard the sirens of the motor-bicycles, he stood up and made a gesture to the Chief of Police, then the police all round the ring leaned over the *barrera* and shouted to call the attention of the attendants. The last bull had just been brought in, and they had to send out a steer to coax him back to the corral, but finally the ring was cleared and the servants threw down handfuls of fresh sawdust and sprinkled the arena with water.

The General came in with a party of officers, each of whom appeared to be wearing a different kind of uniform. The band struck up. The crowd rose to its feet and screamed in hard-voiced ecstasy. It was some minutes before the clamour died down.

"He is quite a small man," Maria said.

There was not room for all the officers in the reserved boxes and they spilled over into the adjoining boxes, the occupants standing immediately to give them seats. The President stood up and held both his hands high for silence. After a few minutes there was complete silence save for a woman's voice in the distance. She was singing the *Conte Jonda*, the traditional wailing song of Andalusia:

"I felt death approach. . . ."

I shot an involuntary glance at Maria.

"It has no significance," Maria said, smiling. "It is sung upon all ceremonious occasions. Behold it, they recommence."

The band had struck up. The ceremonial march had begun again. The three matadors led, their heads up, their free arms swinging. They were very fine in their brocaded cloaks and scarlet pants. Manuel, as was fitting, marched in the centre position. Behind the matadors came the bandilleros, and behind them the picadors. The bandilleros and the picadors were dressed in colours as splendid as the matadors, but the quality of their clothes was not as good. The ring attendants came last of all. They too were dressed in bright colours, and they too marched with dignity. The procession circled the ring and came to a stop before the President's box. The matadors bowed, holding their hats on, and the General made the gesture of approval.

Manuel came over to the *barrera* beside us and handed up his formal cape. I leaned down and took it from him and gave it to Maria, who was already holding his first cape, the one he had presented to her after the inaugural procession.

I wished him luck. "*Mucha suerte.*"

"*Gracias,*" he said, but he looked only at his wife. After a minute he turned away, spoke to his sword-bearer, and then walked slowly to the middle of the ring.

"I think suddenly there is something that I do not like," Maria said to me. I knew what she meant. It is a feeling that I always get when I am waiting for the bull to come out. It is a feeling that constricts your chest even when you do not know the matador. It is a feeling that must be pretty awful for the matador's wife, and on this occasion the feeling was intensified by the presence of the General and by the unleashed hysteria of the people. It was pretty damned awful for me, too.

"Manuel has kept himself in training," I said. "He was fine with the first two bulls."

"It is not that," she said.

The bull came out in a rush, and dug in all four feet and the dust rose to his flanks.

"They have changed the bull," Ramon said. "Look, Mamma, he is a wicked one. We shall see some fun !"

"They have certainly changed the bull," Maria said.

"What would you say that he weighs, this bull ?" Miguel asked. Miguel was only six. "Would you say that he weighs forty *arrobas* ? Would you, Ramon ?"

"No," Ramon said. "About thirty."

When Manuel moved, the bull saw him and charged. He was a young, strong bull, and he did not abide by the book. He had a vicious habit of sheering in the act of taking the cape as if he were allowing for aim-off. With an unconventional bull like this it is very hard for even a great *torrero* to do the conventional things that are expected of him. It is like fighting a bull who watches a man's feet. No bull has ever been known to watch a man's feet only, and that—the *torreros* say—is fortunate, for it would be suicide to fight such a bull.

After the third charge you could see that Manuel had placed the bull in his mind, and knew, it seemed, with mathematical precision exactly what this bull could and could not do.

Manuel's style was austerely classical and stylised. He never gave ground, and he worked without flourishes or unnecessary movements of any kind. He did not make bull-fighting look dangerous. He made it look very simple and inevitable. Watching Manuel was like watching a ballet in slow motion. He had so much control that he made even the bull's clumsy lunges look rehearsed.

In the end he brought the bull over in front of our box for the kill, but first he slowed it with a brilliant series of *veronicas* and *half-veronicas*.

"He is working too close, but is he not beautiful?" Maria said.

"My father always works close up in the bull's terrain," Miguel said. "He never gets *cogida*."

In the *half-veronica* the bull was passing so close under Manuel's arm that the horn was piercing his shirt, and now when he pivoted, raising his arm to give the last flick of the *muleta* that drew the bull through, the torn ribbons of shirting streamed on the bull's back and we could see the brown flesh on Manuel's ribs.

The crowd maintained absolute silence save for the deep satisfied ah-h in the split second that the bull passed Manuel's body.

"I wish that he would kill now," Maria said.

I stole a glance at the Great Man. It was clear that the General was absorbed. He was, I reflected, enjoying his command performance, and I felt bitter again and momentarily angry with Manuel. The crowd caught its breath, and I saw that Manuel had drawn his sword from the *muleta* and was about to kill. He stood on tip-toe, his legs firm, and, holding the blade at a slight angle, sighted along his bent left arm. When the bull came he took the impact without any movement of his feet, and it was only when he had stopped the bull and the sword was in the shoulder up to the hilt that he stepped clear. It was the perfect kill. He turned away without interest before the bull fell, and walked over to the *barrera*. He put both his hands on the *barrera* and leaned like that, his arms at full length, for a second, then he looked up at Maria.

When the bull fell, the crowd went crazy. They threw flowers into the ring and everyone waved handkerchiefs. I saw the General himself wave. Even the picadors and the ring-servants were smiling. The bull had turned over on his left side, and they had to lever him up and tug on the hilt, their feet on the bull's shoulder, to withdraw the sword. They wiped it clean and brought it to Manuel, who was still staring up at his wife in a way that I could not understand.

The crowd roared. Everyone was standing.

Manuel drew the sword carefully through his *muleta*, then, holding it in the correct formal manner, walked across to the President's box where the General sat wreathed in smiles of condescension and the officers nodded amiably to each other in critical appreciation.

Manuel bowed and the General nodded twice. Then Manuel held up his left hand and let the cape fall, and there was immediate silence. It was a silence of utter amazement. The ceremony of the *Corrida* is strictly conventional, and to the vast audience this action by Manuel was an inconceivable breach of etiquette. I heard the scuff of the cape as it hit the ground.

"I have given you the bull," Manuel said suddenly, throwing back his head and using a firm clear voice that was audible through the whole plaza. "Now I give Spain my life. I die, but I die for the glory of a *free* Spain. *Viv'España!*"

He placed the sword deliberately against his heart, and, holding the hilt with both hands, fell forward on it. His legs did not even twitch.

"*Muerto!*" Maria said in a puzzled voice. "He is dead."

6

Afterwards, I understood many things. I understood that Manuel Garcio had not been altogether indifferent to the issues at stake in the Spanish War, and I understood something of the absurd, magnificent pride that had driven him to this final act which alone among all the acts of war accorded in his mind with the dignity of a great *torrero*. I realised that he had planned this last dramatic gesture many months, perhaps years, before, and I realised also that he had had a very good reason for telling me of the uncle and aunt in Puente Genil who had such an affection for his Maria. He had undoubtedly made all his dispositions with great care. His affairs were in excellent order.

There was one thing, however, that he had not provided against. Confiscation. I do not think it had occurred to him that his estate and his capital might be confiscated, but that, of course, is what happened.

The edict was promulgated on the evening of the day he died, the same evening that I took Maria and the children to the house of Señor Priego, the evening I began to paint the picture that I called "Portrait of Manuel."

I would like to be able to tell you that the critics agreed on the greatness of my "Portrait of Manuel," and that I sold it for a great deal of money. This is not the case, however.

There was a British contingent on the boat I caught at Lisbon. Half a dozen journalists, the representative of a wine firm, a banker, two Naval officers who had been attached to the Embassy, and—don't ask me why—a small-time theatrical producer. They were all jolly good fellows, all in high spirits, all glad to be going home, all happy because the war was over at last and the suffering at an end and everything in the Anglo-Spanish garden so lovely.

I suppose that I was happy too.

Anyway, I got very merry at a party the night before we docked at Southampton and gave the "Portrait of Manuel" to my cabin steward, who had said it was real pretty, although he hadn't the faintest idea what it was all about.

When I woke, the ship was tied up at Southampton and the steward had already been discharged. I got his address and finally tracked him down in Liverpool, where he lied to me that he could not remember what he had done with the painting. I think he must have got worried when he saw how determined I was to find it, because he wrote to me afterwards confessing that he had not had room for it in his trunk and had thrown it over the side.

I took it hard at the time. It really was a great painting. It was the kind of job you do only once in a lifetime.

MY FRIEND JOSEPH

F IRST: HOW I MET HIM.
I had gone to Manchester to see my father. To ask my father
for money. I wanted the money so that I could marry Lizzie
and save her from a fate worse than death. Yes, that was how I
thought of it. I was twenty-one.

"Tell me about her, then," my father said, sitting stiff-backed
behind his desk. "How old is she, and what about her family?"

He had me there of course.

"She's nearly eighteen," I said.

"And her family?"

"She can't help her family. And anyway, they're mostly dead."

"What does she do?"

"Well," I said, "she's a sort of a kind of a maid. To Jacobus.
Jacobus, the boxing manager, and Mrs. Stevens. Mrs. Stevens
is his housekeeper." I knew how it sounded. It sounded terrible.
"But you don't understand," I said. "She's different. Really she
is, Dad. She's a wonderful girl."

"Son," my father said, "the world is full of wonderful girls,
especially the first one." As he spoke he placed his hand on a
sheaf of papers, raised his first two fingers, and drummed

con spirito, as we said at home. I knew what this meant. It meant that the subject was closed.

"Then you won't help me?"

"No, son," my father said.

I went out and walked the streets. I walked for a long time, along streets that I did not know and would not know again, and finally I walked into a fairground. I saw the notice that said MURPHY'S FAMOUS BOXING BOOTH, and I paid my sixpence and walked under the notice into the tent. I stood on my toes and, looking down an avenue of cloth caps, saw a large ugly white man hit a large ugly black man on the chin. It was a notable punch. It travelled only a few inches, but it wrenched the negro's chin up from his chest, spun him half around, and sent him crashing like timber.

Gus, my boss in Sports, once told me always look at their heels, so I looked then at the negro's heels, and saw that they were flat on the boards and that his toes were up. "If their heels are flat," Gus said, "that's that." And so it was of course.

"The Pole the winner!" the referee said. "The killer diller!"

The crowd did not like it. They had paid for ten rounds and got only one. They thought they had been cheated and they said so, with emphasis. They were still booing when the negro was carried from the ring, and they saved a special raspberry for the winner as he ducked through the ropes and, grinning, nodding, and shaking hands with himself, made for the canvas flap marked *Dressing-room*. He appeared to be pleased with his reception. He actually seemed to think that he was popular. I watched him till he disappeared from sight, and then, smelling a story, I elbowed across the tent to the partitioned-off section, raised the canvas flap, and peered into the Dressing-room.

The negro lay almost at my feet. Two men in sweaters were

working on him, slapping his face and hands, while a third sluiced him with water from a bucket. The Pole was over in the corner farthest from me. He was surrounded by a jostling mill of small men of the kind you always find around a boxing booth, and he was busy lifting these spivs two at a time and banging their heads together.

It was hard to know just what was going on. Everybody, except the negro, was shouting at the top of his voice, and everybody, especially the Pole, was in a very bad temper. The little rat-faced referee had a restraining hand on the elastic waistband of the Pole's pants, but that wasn't stopping the Pole. When he saw me he dropped his victims and came at me, and there was no time for me to go. He came the direct way, stepping over the negro's torso, and he came fast.

"You see William?" he demanded.

"I don't understand."

"William is his bird," Ratface said. "His magpie."

"You see her?" the Pole said, grabbing my coat lapels.

"No," I said.

"For the love of God," Ratface said to the roof. "Sweet God, will somebody please find William!"

Well, that was the first time I met the Pole.

When I got back to London there was a dearth of news, and I slapped out a bit about Murphy's Famous Boxing Booth. Gus let the stuff through, and I had two small pars in each of the evening editions and one in the morning paper.

Next day I had a phone call from Jacobus.

"Hullo," I said. "Hullo, Mr. Jacobus." I cleared my throat to catch hold of my voice and waited. I was thoroughly scared. I thought of course that he had found out about Lizzie and me. I thought he knew it was me who had kept her out late the night before.

"Listen," Jacobus said. "Somebody in your paper wrote about a Pole. What I want to know is this. Is he good, this Pole? I mean *good*."

"He's wonderful," I said. "He's sensational, Mr. Jacobus." Now I did not think that the Pole was so very good. When I spoke I did not think of the Pole at all. I thought only of keeping Jacobus sweet, and I just opened my mouth and said what I knew he would like best to hear.

"You think he's worth looking at, boysie?"

"I certainly do, Mr. Jacobus," I said.

And that was how Jacobus came to sign up the Pole. That was the start of it all.

2

I went along to the Gym. (Jacobus's Boxing Academy) the day after the Pole arrived. I went in the hope of catching a glimpse of Lizzie, but I let it be known that I had come to see the Pole. I stood and watched him at the heavy bag for a few minutes, then I stepped across to the plywood office to pay my respects to Jacobus.

"Well, how do you like him, Mr. Jacobus?" I asked.

"All right," Jacobus said. "But he don't talk. I paid good money for him, and what I say is I got the right to have him talk to me. You tell him that, boysie. Tell him he's got to behave hisself when he's here and talk when he's talked at. So far he don't talk to nobody at all, not even the boys, but you tell him that, like I said, boysie. Maybe he'll listen to you."

So I talked to the Pole.

"Hullo," I said. "How are you getting on?"

The Pole scowled and hit the bag with a double left hook.

"You like it here?" I asked.

The Pole hit the bag again, one-one-two, and he hit to hurt.

"How's William?" I said.

The Pole stepped back and looked at me. He had stopped scowling, and was wearing what I took to be an eager and a friendly look, but it hadn't done his face any good at all. I don't know if there are words to fit the Pole's face. It was very big and very, very ugly. When you first looked at it you got the impression that it had more bones in it than necessary, that these bones were bigger than human bones, and that they were not in the places where they ought to be. But after a bit you got accustomed to the idea of the Pole's face, and when you looked at it you didn't see it. You saw only his eyes. His eyes were okay. They were no different from anybody else's eyes, and I think they were brown.

"You know William?" he said.

"Not exactly," I said. "But I know about him. Did you ever find him?"

"No," the Pole said.

That was the sum total of words spoken. I did not think that I had done very well, but Jacobus was impressed. "You made a hit," he said. And later, when he had thought it over, he called me into the office. "Listen, boysie," he said, "do me a favour. You come and talk to him as often as you can, and some night you take him out. Will you do that for old Jacobus? There's no one else can start him talking, and it gets you down, that frozen puss—just take a look at it—my God, I seen ugly pans, but I never seen the like a that; you're his friend, you come along and take him out some night, make him laugh. Will you do that, boysie? I'll pay expenses."

"I'll be glad to oblige you, Mr. Jacobus," I said. I always said yes to Jacobus. I knew that he was harmless. I knew that he was cheap and crooked and contemptible, and I used often to lie in bed at night and work out the way I would treat him the next time we met. The way I would treat him would be like dirt. I decided on it definitely, yet when I got face to face with him I always remembered that he was Lizzie's guardian and that he had Rags Gorman behind him (that especially) and I always got a tight feeling in my stomach and I always went out of my way to be very polite and agreeable, and I nodded my head and said yes, Mr. Jacobus, no matter what Jacobus said. "Certainly, I'll take him out, Mr. Jacobus," I said. "What's his name?"

"God knows," Jacobus said. "I ain't thought one up yet. Now you take him to a cinema, see. Nothing flashy. And, boysie, no eats. He gets that at his place. Board and lodgings. Comprehensive. Good solid food. I got that all fixed. Just some little cinema place."

I called for the Pole at the Gym. at six the following evening.

Lizzie knew that I was due, and came down the stairs with something for the garbage tin, but Jacobus was there, and she would not look at me although she waggled her skirt, meaning affection. I was ashamed to walk with the Pole because of the way everyone stared, and I was angry with Lizzie for not having looked me once in the eyes. I didn't say a word, and I thumbed the Pole into the first cinema I saw. The main film was a marriage comedy with Melvyn Douglas and a blonde, I don't remember her name. It was a very funny film in parts, and I had to laugh, and when I laughed the Pole laughed too. He had a terrible laugh, like something in an opera.

When it was all over I walked the Pole home. I tried to make conversation in basic English and the Pole listened gravely, saying "Please?" and "Yes, thank you," these at the wrong times, and precious little else. We finished the last half-mile in silence, and I was mighty relieved when we came to his lodgings. I thumbed out the door to him in case he hadn't the sense to know where he lived.

"Well, so long," I said.

The Pole took my hand, shook it hard, and bowed.

"Thank you, pet," he said.

I didn't have to think that out. It was straight from the film. Melvyn to his wife. *Thank you, pet*. It certainly rocked me back on my heels. I could not think of an appropriate reply, and I was determined not to laugh. I merely said, "So long, then," and turned away. I looked back from the street corner and saw that the Pole was still standing at the door. When he saw me looking, he raised his hat and bowed again, and I giggled and shot quickly round the corner.

Thank you, pet!

That big gorilla.

Oh, it amused me. It gave me a fine laugh, but it also made me realise that the Pole was a human being, and now, when I look back at it, it does not seem at all funny. It seems sad.

3

The Pole, registered as Joseph Hamilton (Hamilton was Mrs. Stevens's middle name: Mrs. Stevens was Jacobus's house-keeper), K.O.'d his first two opponents in the third and first rounds respectively, and Jacobus, who believed a pound in the hand was worth ten in the offing, rushed him into a match with Al Kid Williams of Cardiff, who was good. I didn't like it at all. I had grown fond of Joseph. I had started him off on night classes, taken him twice to Bertram Mills, walked him interminably round the Zoo. I had got used to the big cuss, and

I didn't want to see him cut to ribbons. I knew that this so-called fight could only be a massacre, and I would have stopped it if I could. But I couldn't. The contract was signed and the bills were up before I even learned of it. AL KID WILLIAMS v. BIG JOE HAMILTON. It was to be a ten-round supporting bout at Blackfriars, and the Pole was given what Jacobus described as "an extensive preparation." This included beef tea twice daily and a punch-drunk sparring partner. Joseph, reeking of embrocation, showed me his muscles and his secret left jab. He seemed perfectly content with his new existence, and I was fool enough to think that he was settling down.

Then, six days before the fight, he disappeared.

I met Lizzie on the evening of that day in the Public Library where we had a standing date, Wednesdays, and she told me about it out of the corner of her mouth. Joseph had not turned up at the Gym. that morning, his bed had not been slept in, his landlady had not seen him since the previous day. The boys were all out searching. They were combing the parks and the river-banks. They had divided the city into sectors, and in their various sectors they were taking in all the pubs, the police offices, the hospitals and the mortuaries. Jacobus was up to high doh, and when last seen was sitting purple at the tele-phone, working through the Directory. Lizzie wanted me to think where Joseph could be, but I could not think, and I did not want to waste our precious time together. I jockeyed her round to the Archæology Stall.

Nine days out of ten we could count on getting the Archæ-ology Stall to ourselves, but this had to be one of the tenth days. An old man in a black reefer coat was seated on the ladder stool taking notes. Lizzie and I pretended to look at the books. We brushed hands and exchanged glances. We waited for a long time for the old man to move, but the old man sat on like a fixture, and at last Lizzie said desperately with her eyes that she had to go.

"Not unless," I said.

"But him."

"Him or no him," I whispered. "I mean it."

Lizzie bit her lip, considering this. "All right," she said at last.

So I kissed her.

That was the first time we ever kissed in public. The old man was not watching us, and maybe it is not strictly correct to speak of a single unmindful old man as public, but that was how I thought of him. I thought, "This is the first time I have ever kissed her in public," and because of that thought that kiss became a very special one, and even now, after an interval of more than ten years, I exactly remember it. Lizzie was wearing a new and unfamiliar perfume, and I have no doubt that it was a very cheap perfume, that she had too much of it on, and that it smelled terrible, but it smelled like a million dollars to me, and it still does. Just before she slipped out of my arms she jerked in closer than she had ever been before, holding very tightly, and when she did so her breasts jellied and took up a new position against my chest. It was a moment of excruciating beauty.

She pushed me away very soon, but I caught at her hand and would not let her go. I had a question to ask her. It was a very important question, and I asked it every time I saw her.

"Lizzie," I whispered. "What about Rags Gorman?"

"What about him?"

"You know, Lizzie. Has he been at you again?"

"He hasn't been near the house for a week."

"Truly?"

"Cross my heart."

"Thank God," I said. I was mightily pleased. I was light-headed with relief. I felt as brisk and jaunty as a bee, and for the time being I forgot all about Joseph and Joseph's strange disappearance.

.　　.　　.　　.　　.　　.

Next morning Jacobus was in the office at 9.30 a.m. Later, when Joseph was winning fights, he was Jacobus's boy, now he was my thattaty-that Pole. Jacobus was very high. He was talking in terms of the front page. He wanted posters and photographs and headlines, and he wanted them NOW. This was not my class of business, so I took him to Gus. I doubt if it was Gus's class of business either, but Jacobus could never have guessed that. Gus picked a cigarette off the back of his ear, lighted it carefully, put his hands on his stomach, and listened. Gus was fat and old and cynical, and nobody ever would stampede Gus.

"Is this the gorilla you told me about?" Gus said to me. "This Pole?"

"Yes, Gus."

"Well, we'll do what we can, Mr. Jacobus," Gus said.

That wasn't enough for Jacobus, though. Jacobus wanted a nation-wide search for the Pole. He wanted sandwich-men. He wanted front-page photographs and finger-size headlines. Jacobus wanted the moon. He talked quick and fast and very big, and as Gus did not interrupt him he got louder and bigger and more and more important. He got so important that he quite forgot himself and even went so far as to say that he would offer a reward.

"How much?" Gus snapped, quick as a ferret.

Jacobus shut his mouth with a click and subsided to his usual size. "How much?" he said warily. "How *much*? Well,

222

just say a reward. You don't have to mention the exact cash. Leave that to me. Say, you boys don't mebbe think I'm a piker, do you? I'm no piker. No, sirs!" And he snatched a wad of greasy notes from his pocket and slapped it on the desk. "Money's no object with Jacobus," he said. "Just take a look at that." But we had time only to catch a glimpse of the wad before he swooped on it, two-handed, and thrust it back into his pocket.

Well, we put a photograph of Joseph in the Sports page and ran a feature story, MISSING HEAVYWEIGHT, and one or two of the other papers carried a similar story, but nothing came of any of them, nobody wrote or rang Jacobus to say that they had seen the Pole, and so one day passed and half of another; then, on the evening of the next day, Saturday that was, I walked out of the office door right into Joseph's arms. (Harry the door-keeper told me afterwards that he had been hanging around for hours.) When I say that I walked into Joseph's arms I mean just that. He picked me up nose-high, shook me till I rattled, and shouted gleefully across the inch that separated our faces.

"Come home," he said, grinning. "Home with me."

I tried to question him, but it was no good. Joseph had room for only one idea at a time, and when it was an urgent idea like this one he just plugged it, and kept on plugging it.

"Home," he shouted, giving me another playful shake. "Home. See John!"

So I went home with him. So I saw John.

John was seated in a cardboard box in the middle of the Pole's bed. John was a bird. I learned afterwards that he was a Blue Abyssinian Duck and extremely valuable, but I did not know that at the time. He was a medium-sized greyish bird with bright blue wings and a white diamond patch on his head, and he squawked like a goose. When I took a couple of steps into the room, he stood up and beat his wings at me. The Pole chk-chkd at him, lifted him and put him on his shoulder, and John sat quiet.

I stared at them and they stared back at me, unblinking, and I swear they both had wide grins on their incredible faces. I gave up, and sat down on the bed.

Jacobus said he had always suspected that the Pole was mad. Now he knew for certain. "After the Williams fight I'll throw the big ape out on his ear," he said. He did not say this to me. He said it to Mrs. Stevens in Lizzie's presence, and Lizzie told me. "But meantime I got to keep him from getting lost again, and the only way to make sure of that is to have him here in the house with us."

"Sleeping?" Mrs. Stevens said.

"Sleeping," Jacobus said.

"And the bird?" Mrs. Stevens enquired.

"The bird, too, I suppose. It's only till the fight. Only for a couple of days."

"I'll have you know, Mr. Jacobus," Mrs. Stevens said, "that I'll have no bloody bird in my house. And that, Mr. Jacobus, is final." Mrs. Stevens always called Jacobus Mr., and Jacobus had to call her Mrs. too, even in bed. That was the sort of woman Mrs. Stevens was. Exceedingly proper. Jacobus had taken her on as housekeeper in Lizzie's mother's place when Lizzie's mother died, and Mrs. Stevens had never forgiven Lizzie, and never would, for being the daughter of her predecessor. She had so strong a sense of propriety that she even thought it indecent that Lizzie and she should be sleeping under the same roof, and she said so several times a day.

She was a big red-haired woman, handsome enough, I suppose, with an outstanding bosom and a wide muscular mouth which she used from morning to night, mostly on Lizzie. She was at pains to tell everyone that she did not wish Lizzie any harm. All she wished was that Lizzie was dead or settled in an institution or teamed up with Rags Gorman. Rags Gorman the bookie, who, only a few years ago, had been hawking rags in the streets and who now wore a coat with an astrakhan collar and financed all the racketeers in the district, Jacobus included. It was Mrs. Stevens, not Jacobus, who kept throwing Lizzie at Rags Gorman's head. It was Mrs. Stevens who had first got the idea that Rags needed a "housekeeper" and that Lizzie was just the girl for the job. Give Jacobus his due, he didn't much like this idea. He never actually got the length of opposing it, he was too scared of Rags Gorman, and I guess he was scared of Mrs. Stevens too, but he played for time, he said, "Wait till she's eighteen," and he came right out in the open over the new clothes that Mrs. Stevens wanted to buy Lizzie for bait. He argued for a week, and in the end he said, "All right. The costume. But not the fancy underclothes." Mrs. Stevens said the underclothes were the most important of all. She kept on at him about it, and each day when I saw Lizzie she told me how it was going; it was like a running commentary on a fight, with Jacobus always backing away, ducking and weaving, and Mrs. Stevens chasing him all round the ring but unable to land a decisive blow. Lizzie wanted the underclothes, of course, but I didn't want her to have them. I couldn't sleep at nights and I prayed like I never prayed for or against any other thing that Lizzie wouldn't get those underclothes, and she didn't. Jacobus finally stood his ground. He said No. Every now and again when he got really cornered he said no to Mrs. Stevens, but for every time he said no he said yes a hundred times or more, and even when he insisted on getting his own way he made a point of giving Mrs. Stevens a bit of her own way too, to keep her sweet. Like over Joseph and the bird, for instance.

Joseph was duly installed in the spare bedroom (Jacobus). The bird was locked in the loft over the Gym. (Mrs. Stevens).

.　　.　　.　　.　　.

The day before the Williams fight Gus called me to his desk and put his finger on a paragraph in *The Evening News*. This paragraph stated that a bird, a valuable Blue Abyssinian Duck, had disappeared from St. James's Park.

" 'Any person having any information,' " Gus said, reading, " 'please communicate with the Keeper of St. James's Park or with any police station.' That person, my boy, is you."

It always was me when there was trouble and the Pole was in it. Well, I waited till after the fight. It was this fight which put the Pole on the map, because to everyone's amazement (especially Jacobus's) he won in the fifth round, knocking out Al Kid Williams with as vicious a left uppercut as even Gus had ever seen. I waited till the morning after the fight, and then I tackled Joseph about the Blue Abyssinian Duck.

I was very severe. I gave him a long lecture, in the course of which I told him in a dozen different ways that it was wrong to steal. I kept it very simple. I said that John was not Joseph's bird: John was the public's bird. And so on. "So you've got to take him back to where you found him," I said finally.

"Why?" Joseph said.

I began all over again. I took it in steps. Each short sentence was a step, and at the end of each step I said, "Do you understand?" and each time Joseph said, "Yes," so I worked up to the climax and said firmly, "So there it is. You have to take him back to the Park, Joseph."

Joseph fidgeted and hung his head.

226

"Why?" Joseph said.

This might have gone on for a long time if I had not hit on a simplification. "Joseph," I said, "I think you know about the King, don't you?"

"Yes," Joseph said, bowing.

"Well," I said, "John belongs to the King."

"God Save the King," Joseph said.

There was no more argument. That same night Joseph and I took a ride up West to St. James's Park, and some time around midnight the King got back his duck.

4

Joseph's next escapade was far more serious.

It took place in September, after Joseph had beaten Tiger O'Malley and Vince Hammett, and while Jacobus was busy edging him into line for a crack at the British title. I was mixed up in all his troubles, but unfortunately I did not take them seriously. I had my own troubles at the time. Rags Gorman was beginning to put the screw on Lizzie, and I was half-crazed with worry; I was sleeping only an hour or two a night, and I was negotiating desperately for a job on a Union paper. If I got a job on a Union paper they would have to pay me a living wage and I could marry Lizzie then and cock a snook at Jacobus, and Rags Gorman too. I thought endlessly of ways and means to land this job, I just hadn't time to waste on Joseph, and I have to admit that I never really bothered about him or his affairs until after the killing, and then it was too late, of course, nobody could do anything for him then.

When Jacobus told me about Joseph's new pet I flatly disbelieved him. I thought he had been drinking.

"You're joking, Mr. Jacobus," I said. "Surely you must be joking!"

"Do I look like I'm joking?" Jacobus said.

He didn't. He looked like a man who is having trouble with his blood pressure. His face was purple, there were veins throbbing on his forehead, and his lips hacked and sawed at each other.

"He's got a lion all right," he said, nodding. He was making a great effort at self-control. He spoke with only a small part of his voice and dropped each word separately, like a penny in a slot. "A live lion," he said. "And what's more, he's got it in my loft, and he's up there with it now."

I saw that I was expected to say something, perhaps even to do something. I said helplessly, "Where did he get it, Mr. Jacobus?"

"He says he found it."

"Where?"

"I think," Jacobus said, showing his teeth like a rat, "that he found it on a bus."

That was Joseph's story, and he stuck to it. I tried him hard, but he would tell no other. He was scared, but resolute. I talked to him like a Dutch uncle. I told him he could not possibly keep a lion, and I told him why. Joseph fixed his eyes on a spot several feet above my shoulder and shook his head at it. "This lion is a dog," he said.

I consulted Jacobus. "He says it's a dog," I told him.

"He's a liar," Jacobus said. "It's a lion and nothing but a lion. You see it."

So I saw the animal. It was a lion all right. I don't know a lot about lions, and I was content to see this one briefly through a chink in the loft door, but at a guess I would say it was about a year-old lion. It hadn't quite filled out; nevertheless, it was an ugly customer. It was the size of a big Alsatian dog and certainly lion enough to do damage.

I talked to Joseph till I ran short of saliva. He listened politely, and when I had finished he said, as far as I could make out, that he would do anything on earth for me, yea gladly, anything else, but he would not give up the lion.

"I love this lion," he said.

That was probably true. I knew by this time that Joseph had a great capacity for loving all God's creatures, and I had to admit that it was possible that Joseph really did love this lion, as much perhaps as I loved Lizzie, although in a different way of course. I did not know what to say, and, not knowing, I got angry and argued. I should have known better than try to argue with Joseph. "You can't possibly love a lion. Be sensible," I said. "The lion is one of the fiercest of all the beasts. It's a man-eating carnivore. It eats human beings. Do you understand that?" I made the motions with my mouth. "Eats them."

"This lion has a soft mouth," Joseph said.

"No lion has a soft mouth," I said. "Think of the danger, man." I thought of it myself. "My God," I said.

"This lion has a soft mouth and there is no danger," Joseph said.

I pointed out in elaborate detail just how much danger there was.

"Not with this lion, Robert," Joseph said. "And this lion's nice soft mouth."

I got mad then, and I spoke in a way that I had never spoken to him before. I spoke to hurt, and I did hurt him. I was savage and sarcastic. I really let myself go, and for good measure I threw in a home truth or two that was not strictly to the point. Joseph hung his head and trembled like a monstrous, miserable child. I couldn't go on shouting at him. I checked myself and clapped him on the arm. "Now, Joseph," I said gently, "be sensible."

He raised his head and looked at me, and his eyes were like a whipped dog's.

"You'll get over it, Joseph," I said.

He shook his head. He sagged.

And then the idea hit him. It hit him quite visibly, like a kidney punch. He straightened up, his face jerked to life, and he thrust his hand to his mouth and pulled out his new plate of artificial dentures, a legacy from the O'Malley fight. "See, Robert," he said, brandishing this plate at me. "No danger with my lion. My lion has false teeth, like me!"

There wasn't much you could do with a clown like that.

I went down to the Gymnasium and told Jacobus what the Pole had told me. Jacobus didn't think it funny. He threw a newly lighted cigarette to the floor and screwed it into shreds with the heel of his patent-leather shoe. "I'll fix him," he said, simmering. He lifted his foot and looked at the remains of the cigarette in a sudden new passion. "The big suching so-and-so," he said. "I'll fix him, see if I don't."

.   .   .   .   .   .

Jacobus did not fix the Pole, however. At least not immediately.

The truth is, Jacobus was afraid of the Pole. The Pole never spoke to Jacobus, and when he looked at Jacobus he scowled. I didn't blame Jacobus for being scared. If the Pole had scowled every time he looked at me I would have been scared too.

Well, Jacobus waited.

He had good reason to wait, because just at this time he was engaged in a very delicate piece of fiddling. The British Board of Boxing Control was about to examine the question of

Joseph's nationality and had summoned Joseph and Jacobus to appear before it at the end of the month. Jacobus had got documents from Rags Gorman's lawyer which purported to prove that Joseph was British, but all the documents in the world would not be enough if Joseph himself chose to be awkward. (*Unco-operative* was the word the lawyer used.)

Now Jacobus knew perfectly well that if he took Joseph's lion away from Joseph the odds were that Joseph would be extremely unco-operative. The result would be unfortunate. The Board would decide that Joseph was not eligible to fight for the British title and he, Jacobus, would lose a nice fat purse. In the circumstances he could not afford to be on worse than scowling terms with Joseph. He therefore decided, according to Lizzie, to sit tight and do nothing at all about the lion—*meantime*. He merely bought Mrs. Stevens a fur cape, presented the Pole with a reinforced bar and padlock for the loft door, and settled down to wait till the British Boxing Board of Control gave their decision. "By the Lord God," he swore, "I'll fix him then."

"What's he going to do?" I asked.

"Tell the police," Lizzie said.

.   .   .   .   .   .

The Board met on the last day of September. The stewards asked Joseph questions on which Joseph had not been primed, and Joseph could not answer these questions.

"Although he's pure British," Jacobus said, "the truth is, he don't understand English so good."

After discussion the stewards decided to examine Joseph with the aid of an interpreter, and the meeting was duly adjourned for three weeks. During these three weeks Jacobus signed a contract (provisional on the Board's decision) for a twelve-round championship elimination fight at Harringay between Joseph and Jackie Wilson, the official contender; and some time also during these three weeks Joseph, spruced and nervous, came to the office to consult me on a personal matter of great importance.

We talked in the corridor outside the Reporters' Room.

"I have troubles," Joseph said.

Joseph's troubles were small beer compared with those of everyone around him. Joseph's troubles were purely financial. He wanted more money for the coming fight. He told me this in a very roundabout way, and while he spoke he jigged from one leg to the other and raised his eyes only as far as my knees.

"I want a lot of money," he said.

"How much?" I asked.

"Twenty pounds."

"Let's get this straight," I said. "Do you want twenty pounds more than you've been getting or twenty pounds in all?"

"All of twenty pounds," Joseph said. "In my hand."

His eyes crept up and touched me warily in the face. "Is it reasonable, Robert?"

He was perfectly serious. I took a deep breath and let it out slowly. I asked him what money he had been getting from Jacobus.

"A five pound," Joseph said. "Each fight a five pound. I want twenty. Is it reasonable?"

"My God," I said. I just couldn't believe that even Jacobus was as mean as that. I stared helplessly at the Pole, and he fidgeted and dropped his eyes back where they had come from. I realised that he was waiting for me to tell him whether his request for twenty pounds was reasonable, and I realised also that I had not yet heard the whole of this story. "What do you want the twenty pounds for?" I asked.

"To buy a cow."

"A what?"

"A cow," Joseph said. "The butcher says I give twenty pounds I get a cow. A whole cow. Dead."

"You mean a carcass?" I said. I began to understand then. "The body of a cow. You want to buy the body of a cow for your lion, is that it?"

"The body of a whole cow," Joseph said. "For twenty pounds. Therefore I want twenty pounds. Is it reasonable?"

"It is reasonable," I had to say.

"Then you come with me," Joseph said, "and speak also to Jacobus, if you please."

So I went with him.

When Jacobus heard what Joseph had to say his eyes got very shifty and he said, "Yes, yes, yes. All right, I said yes, didn't I?"

"I put the rest into gilt-edged for him," he said to me. "He wouldn't know what to do with it, so I save it for him. I put the whole lot into gilt-edged." He was still off balance, for he actually brought out his case and offered me a cigarette. "But boysie," he said. "That's not for printing in your paper."

I had the guts of a cockroach.

"No, no, of course not, Mr. Jacobus," I said.

5

I left Joseph at the Gym. and boarded a number 13 bus at the corner of the street. I was about to go upstairs when I heard Lizzie's voice and, looking round, I saw her racing across the road from the Gymnasium. She ran like a little girl in a hurry, using the whole width of her skirt, her legs showing high-up, and her unbuttoned raincoat streaming from her shoulders.

The bus was already under way.

"Hey, Mac !" I said to the conductor. "Just a minute, please." I grabbed Lizzie by the elbow and hoisted her on to the platform, and Lizzie said, "Phew ! Thought I'd missed you," and leaned for a moment, panting on my chest.

The people in the downstairs were staring, so we went up top. It was quiet up top, and we had the back of the bus to ourselves. "I phoned," Lizzie said. "But they said you weren't at the office. I had to see you."

"Something's happened !" I said, bracing myself.

"Certainly has," Lizzie said. "You'll never guess either. Something pretty terrible. Rags Gorman came last night and they left me alone with him and I had one bit of a time, I can tell you."

I had a landslide in my stomach, and I guess something must also have happened in my face.

"Keep your shirt on," Lizzie said. "I didn't let him get his hands on me, if that's what you're thinking. No, Robert, it was worse than that."

"Worse," I said. "*Worse!*"

"Worse," Lizzie said, nodding. "He actually wants to marry me ! It's not just a line either. He really and seriously wants to marry me. He said it in front of Jacobus and Mrs. Stevens before they left us alone. He said he would come back to-morrow night for his answer, and they've both of them been at me ever since. Jacobus is mad at me for still calling him Mr. Gorman to his face, he's all for it now that Rags is talking marriage, and Mrs. Stevens, you know what she's like, it's been nag, nag, nag, Rags this, Rags that, nothing but Rags all day long, what a gent he is and what a compliment it is to have a really important kind of gent like Rags actually wanting to marry me. In church too, Mrs. Stevens says. Rags never said nothing about church to me, but Mrs. Stevens swears he said it to her. 'Your own mother never had a wedding in her life,' Mrs. Stevens said. You know her. You know how she goes on about that. 'And you—your own mother's daughter . . .' *etcetera*—all that dirt she rakes up—'here's you with an offer from the richest man in the district, a real gentleman, a book-maker, and not only he wants to marry you but in a church too, and look at the house you'll have, and the money, and the respect, folks touching their caps to you in the streets and nobody'll dare not to; my God, it makes me certainly wonder. You bitch,' Mrs. Stevens said, 'you don't deserve it.' "

Lizzie stopped for breath, let her head fall limply on my shoulder, and said, "Oh, Robert dearie, I've had a terrible, hell of a day!"

We sat on the top of that bus for a long time. We went all the way to the terminus, and half of the way back, and we talked continuously, but I don't know that we said very much. I remember I was all for getting married straight away. I said we had to, now. Lizzie said how could we, would I just please kindly tell her how we possibly could when I wasn't even able to keep myself in cigarettes. It was an old argument, and it went on and on. Lizzie was the practical one, and when she was being most practical I always saw a deep strain of idealism in her, deeper than any I possessed, and I always loved her very dearly. I was willing, no, eager, to take a chance on the gutter. But Lizzie wasn't. She knew it too well. She knew what the gutter did to you, and she wasn't going to let it do that dirty thing to me or to the nice clean feeling we had between us.

I tried to be masterful.

I told her that I wasn't going to stand for any more nonsense. I had made up my mind what we were going to do. We were going to get married.

Yes, *married*.

After we were married I would take her up north to my home, and she would live with my father and mother till I could afford to send for her. I said that once my mother got to know her she would love her, and I said that I knew Lizzie would love my mother too, and I made it all sound very convincing, so much so that I almost believed it myself. But Lizzie didn't. She gave me a calm, wise, female smile and shook her head.

She said decisively, "The only thing to do is to tell them to their faces that I'm in love with you. They'll leave me alone then. I'll just tell them the truth, and if they don't like it they can go jump in the river."

We finally agreed on that.

"After all," Lizzie said, "all they can do is get mad at me."

This was not strictly correct. They could, and certainly would, try to prevent her from seeing me again, and they might also bring pressure to bear on me. I reckoned that henceforth I would be a marked man. I would have to watch my step, keep to the lighted streets. I had no illusions about Rags Gorman. I feared him almost as much as I hated him, and I had a great respect for what I thought to be his methods.

I put my arm round Lizzie's shoulders and held her very tight. "Don't worry," I said, lying. "There's really nothing to worry about." She felt extra small and brittle, and I loved her unbearably. "Darling," I said. "Oh, darling, I'll make this up to you some day, I swear I will."

"It's okay," Lizzie said. "Really it is. All this is much worse or you, Robert, than it is for me." And she raised her face to

236

mine and gave me a smile that hit me in the chest and hurt. She was magnificent.

"*I'm* not worrying," she said.

6

The next day was the longest I have ever lived through. Lizzie was to phone in the evening. She was to slip out and ring me whenever she got rid of Rags Gorman, and I sat waiting by the office phone for three interminable hours, from 8 till 11 p.m. A crowd of the boys came in then and sat down at the long reporters' table, and I just couldn't take their bright talk. I sat for a little with my arms on the table and my face hidden in my arms, but I couldn't help raising my head each time the phone rang and the boys guessed that I had a date and started ribbing me, and I felt some sort of wild hysteria coming on. I had to get out. I had to get to Lizzie. I left the office at a run, jumped a number 13 at the traffic lights, and got off just opposite Jacobus's Gymnasium some fifteen minutes later.

It was then exactly twenty-two minutes past eleven, and there was nobody about.

I climbed the yard gate and, keeping to the shadow of the house wall, tiptoed up the flight of stone stairs that led to the kitchen door. I don't know exactly what I meant to do. I hoped to see Lizzie, but if I did not see Lizzie I think I meant to hammer on the door and ask to see Joseph. If Joseph was not in I would ask for Jacobus. Somehow or other I would get into that house, and, once in the house, I would find out what had happened to Lizzie.

I peered through the glass panel in the kitchen door. A

glimmer of light came from the fire in the range, and I saw that the room was empty.

I tried the door.

The door opened, and I stepped inside.

The kitchen led into a narrow hall, flanked with doors. I had never been in the house before, but I knew something of its arrangements from Lizzie. I held my breath deep inside me, and edged across to the room which I thought to be the parlour. As I reached it another door was flung open, Jacobus's voice rattled out into the hall, and a broad band of light slid across the wall and exposed me. I closed my eyes in a kind of convulsion. When I opened them I saw Lizzie standing there in front of me, her hand on her throat. I breathed again and took a step towards her, and as I did so she wheeled round and jerked shut the door of the lighted room, grabbed my sleeve, pulled me a few paces down the corridor, opened another door, and thrust me in.

"Are you crazy?" she said in the dark. She sounded angry.

"I don't know," I said. "I suppose I am. Lizzie, are you all right?"

"Of course I'm all right. Why shouldn't I be all right? What's the matter with you?"

"Rags Gorman?" I whispered.

"He's been and gone." She giggled, and I knew then that she wasn't angry: she was just strung-up, like me. "You'll never believe it. Joseph . . . listen, Robert! . . . Joseph threw him downstairs."

"Joseph what!"

"Threw Rags downstairs," she said. "Yes, he did, and broke his wrist for him too. So now Joseph's gone of course, bag and baggage. And the lion's gone too. You know about the Board, don't you?"

"The Board?" I said, dazed.

"The Boxing Board."

"Oh, was that today?" I said. "I'd forgotten. Today's been such a crazy day. No, I don't know. What happened, Lizzie?"

"They decided Joseph was a foreigner of unknown nationality and they said he couldn't fight for the title. Jacobus was raving mad about it. He was fair hopping. He said Joseph botched the whole thing, and when he came home he phoned the police about the lion and a special truck came up from the Zoo and they took the lion away. Joseph didn't know about it. He was at his elocution class, and when he came home Rags Gorman was here, he had just arrived. We were in the parlour, Rags and me, and we heard Jacobus screaming. You should of heard him, something terrible, he was screaming his head off, and Rags and me went out on to the landing to see what was wrong, and the Pole had Jacobus by the throat, up this high, his feet off the ground, and he threw Jacobus right down the stairs, and then he picked up Rags and shook him like a rat and threw him down the stairs too, and when he threw *him* down the stairs he broke his wrist for him."

I felt the firm rim of an object behind my knees and sat down. It was the bed. I had a hold of Lizzie's hand, and when I sat down she had to sit down too. If I had realised it was Lizzie's bed I probably would not have sat down on it, but I don't know, I might have, I was in a flat spin and capable of almost anything.

"Old Joseph!" I said.

"Shht!" Lizzie whispered, tensing up suddenly and digging her nails into my wrist. "Listen! What's that?"

I listened for noises in the house, but all I heard was the loud beating of my heart and a soft friction sound that seemed to come from Lizzie's knees.

"It's only your stockings rubbing together," I said.

"It must be the way my toes are," Lizzie said, "on the floor." She rearranged her legs, but they didn't stop shaking. I sat holding her hand. I could feel the beat of the blood in her finger-tips, and I was very conscious of her trembling legs. After a little I began to tremble too.

"You oughtn't to have come, Robert," Lizzie said softly.

"I had to," I said. "I had to see that you were all right. Thank God you are all right, Lizzie. You must have had an awful time."

"Oh, that," Lizzie said. "You don't know the half of it yet. You see, I told Rags Gorman I couldn't ever marry him. I said I was in love with somebody else, and when he pestered me to say who it was, do you know who I said? I said Joseph. I knew that Rags and Jacobus were so mad at Joseph over the Boxing Board that they just couldn't get any madder, and so I said it was Joseph I was in love with." And she giggled happily. "What do you think of that? Wasn't that clever of me, sugar?"

"Wonderful," I said. I felt a great surge of relief and an even greater surge of love. I pulled Lizzie to me—she came very easily—and we lost our sitting balance and toppled full-length on the bed. It was a very beautiful and terrible moment, and when I kissed her it was even more so.

I took a grip of myself. I put my hands flat on the bed and took the weight of my body on my arms. "I'll have to go," I said.

Lizzie didn't say anything. She just breathed on me.

"Lizzie!" I whispered.

"U-huh?"

"What if somebody comes in, Lizzie?"

"Nobody'll come in," Lizzie said.

"Are you sure?"

"Quite sure," Lizzie said. "So long as you're here you're safe.

It's when you try to leave that they might catch you. Now that you *are* here you'll just have to stay, that's all. I mean till they go to bed."

"But, Lizzie," I said. "Do you think it's proper?"

Lizzie put her arms up and folded them firmly round my neck. "Don't be silly," she said.

So I stayed.

I stayed for a long time, because, as Lizzie said, we might as well be hung for a sheep as a lamb, and there just wasn't any sense in waiting for Jacobus and Mrs. S. to go to bed if we didn't also wait until they went to sleep.

It was some time around 5 a.m. when Lizzie let me out at the kitchen door.

I walked all the way home, and I guess I walked with a swagger. I waved a good morning to the bakers and the milkmen. I whistled. Sometimes I even sang. All my troubles were miraculously gone, puffed away like dust in the high October wind that swirled my coat around me. For the first time in months I was happy. I hadn't a care in the world.

It was almost daylight when I reached my digs.

My digs were on the second floor of a tenement building. At one time or another there had been a lot of girls in the flats— my own landlady had had four daughters—and the steps were neatly hollowed out in the places where the girls, over many generations, had sat canoodling with their boys. There was an especially comfortable big dent in the top stair but one, and when I reached the bend in the landing I saw that this dent was occupied.

"Robert?" a voice said in the gloom.

"Well, well. Joseph!" I said.

He came bounding down the stairs to meet me. A cone of light fell on to the landing from the 40-watt on the floor above, and we were caught in this light like flies in an upturned wine-glass. I saw every jutting bone in his face, and I saw his eyes.

"Robert," he said. "They took my lion."

"I know, I know, Joseph," I said. I had my first pang of conscience then, for I owed my happiness to Joseph, and I had not thought of Joseph or Joseph's troubles for a long, long time. "Never mind," I said, "you'll get another pet. I know what, Joseph. I'll buy you a dog. A fine, big Alsatian dog. A dog is a much better pet than a lion."

"I don't want a dog," Joseph said. "I am unhappy about my lion, but I came to tell you about another thing. I am very happy about this other thing. It is beautiful and a surprise. Lizzie loves me. Jacobus's Lizzie. She loves me, Robert!"

I stared at him and he stared back at me, grinning, nodding violently, mouthing his words like an apoplectic ape. "Yes, hahaha, yes, yes, yes," he said, stuttering. "She loves me."

I saw him briefly as Jacobus must have seen him, not as a human being at all, but as a Thing—a monstrous and a crazy Thing. I loathed him then, and I wanted him to know it. I thrust my face at him, hating him. "Don't be a fool," I said. "You crazy deformed fool," I said. "Who do you think *you* are for Lizzie to love?"

He didn't understand.

"She loves me, Robert," he said doggedly. "She said so."

"She said so," I said, speaking very coldly and deliberately, "only in order to get rid of Rags Gorman who wanted to marry her. Do you understand that? She wanted to get rid of Rags Gorman, and the only way she could get rid of him was by saying that she loved somebody else, and when she was asked who it was that she loved she had a particular reason for not telling the truth, and so she just said the first name that came into her head and it happened to be yours. In point of fact," I

242

said, "she is in love with me." And I jabbed my thumb into my chest. "Me. Do you understand that?"

He understood all right.

I wish now that he had not understood so well and that I had not seen his face in that moment of his understanding. His face was piteous. He stood stockstill, searching my eyes, and then, sucking his breath into his teeth, he swung away and bolted in a wild, animal-like clatter down the stairs.

When I heard the door slam below I came to my senses. I flung myself at the banister rail and shouted after him. "Joseph," I shouted, "I didn't mean it, not like that."

"Joseph!" I shouted. "Come back!"

But I don't suppose he even heard me.

7

Well, I searched for Joseph everywhere. Everywhere I could think of. The public parks, the Embankment, Rowton House, the Salvation Army Hostels. I searched in all the likely places, and I went on searching day after day, but I did not find Joseph nor anyone who had seen him. Lizzie had the bright idea that he might go to the Zoo to be near his lion, but when we made enquiries at the Zoo they told us the lion was not there. The clerk whom we saw said he thought that some menagerie had claimed the lion. He could not tell us the name of the mena-gerie, but he seemed anxious to oblige, and he said if it was important I could leave my name and address and he would find out and send me a postcard.

"Will you *really*?" Lizzie said.

"Really," the clerk said. "Glad to." He was a tall thin man of about thirty, with very light blue eyes and a nervous tic at one corner of his mouth. He had four beautifully sharpened pencils in his breast pocket, and he looked to be the sort of man you could rely on, not in a crisis, maybe, but in the little things of life. Only, he wasn't. He never sent the postcard, and the result was that I did not learn where Joseph's lion was until three weeks later, when I also learned where Joseph was.

Joseph was in jail.

I read about it in the noon edition of my own paper.

BRUTAL MENAGERIE MURDER, my paper said.

KEEPER KILLED

Tragedy struck Harrap's Menagerie in broad daylight yesterday afternoon, when, as reported fully in our earlier editions, a man gained entry to the lions' cage and was driven into the eating corner by one of the young male lions.

George Gavin Gould, the deceased, a keeper at Harrap's Menagerie, entered the cage and shot the lion through the back of the head. It is alleged that the man then attacked the keeper, raising him above his head and throwing him against the bars of the cage, and that as a result of this attack the keeper sustained injuries which proved fatal.

According to the reports of eye-witnesses, the man made repeated attempts to revive the dead lion. He refused to leave the cage even under the threat of fire-arms, and tear gas had eventually to be used. He then collapsed on the lion's body, and the police, who made the arrest, were unable to disengage his arms from the lion's neck. It is reported that it was necessary to drag both man and lion from the cage and to summon medical assistance to prise loose the man's grip.

This tragic incident took place at three o'clock in the afternoon, and was witnessed by a large crowd of holiday-makers, including many children.

SEE STOP PRESS

The STOP PRESS read:

244

MY FRIEND JOSEPH

SEQUEL TO MENAGERIE MURDER

Sequel to the tragedy at Harrap's Menagerie took place in Maryle-
bone Police Court this morning, when a man was charged with the
wilful murder of George Gavin Gould. He gave his name as Joseph
Hamilton, age unknown, professional boxer, of no fixed abode, and
when asked if he wished to make a statement he said, "He killed my
lion."

How I felt is not of much importance to anyone except
myself, but I would like to say it, just once, and leave it at that.
I felt terrible.

.   .   .   .   .   .

I went to see Joseph in Pentonville as soon as the author-
isation came through. They sat me down at one end of a
long deal table, and after a little they brought Joseph in and sat
him down at the other end. We were asked kindly to keep
our hands on the table, and the warder who asked us this sat
down midway between us.

I had got so used to Joseph's face that I hardly ever noticed
it. Now I took a good look at it. I looked at it as I thought a
juryman would, and I was appalled by what I saw.

It was a horrible face.

The forehead was low and ape-like. The eyes were obscured
by monumental, fist-scarred cheek-bones. The nose had been
broken at the bridge and punched right back into its base; the
nostrils were upturned like a syphilitic's. The mouth was
squint and puffy, and the jaw aggressive and immense. Each
feature, taken separately, was sub-human, and the combination
of these sub-human features was something that had to be seen
to be believed. It was a brutal and degenerate face. It was
undoubtedly the face of a murderer.

245

Joseph saw me staring and put his hand up to his throat. They had taken away his collar and tie, and he thought this was what I was looking at. He told me they had done this for fear he might hang himself.

"They think I'm criminal," he said. His eyes were dark and distressed, the pupils dilated, and they took a hold of mine and clung tight, like lover's eyes. "Me," he said. "Criminal!"

"Nobody could think that who knows you," I said. I talked louder than natural, because I had been thinking precisely this myself, because I was embarrassed and unhappy, and determined to be very much at ease. "Nobody could ever think that, Joseph," I said emphatically. "I have a message from Lizzie. Lizzie sends her love. All your friends are thinking about you. We're all standing by you, Joseph."

"I have no friends," Joseph said.

That was true, of course.

"Except you," Joseph said. "Only you, Robert. The rest is not my friends at all. They say that keeping-man was a good man and I am bad, but he was a bad man and he did a bad thing. You know what he did, Robert? He killed my lion."

"I know, Joseph," I said. "I know. But, Joseph, the lion was going to kill you. He saved your life."

"He killed my lion's life," Joseph said.

"But Joseph . . ."

"No," Joseph said. "Listen, Robert. He killed my lion's life. That was a very bad thing he did."

What could I say? I looked at my hands. I folded up my fingers and stared at the nails.

"Nobody understands. But *you* will understand. Will you please understand, Robert?"

You should have seen his face then.

"Please, Robert."

"All right," I said. I'd have said anything. "All right, Joseph. I'll understand. I promise."

"This then," Joseph said. "A lion is different." He wanted to get it right. There were just certain words that would carry the idea, and he wanted desperately to find those words. He thought very hard. He tested phrases soundlessly on his lips. He stared right into me, scowling, while little beads of sweat gathered on his brow and the big wall clock, inscribed JOYNER EIGHT DAY, ticked our precious seconds away. It was several minutes before he spoke, and then he said something like this.

"They took my lion away. The lion does not understand this. The lion does not know that anything happens except what happens to the lion. The lion does not know that there is anywhere at all except where the lion is. The lion does not know that it has been taken away from me. It thinks that I have been taken away from it. When my lion sees me again it thinks it has found me. It pushes me into a corner. It does not push me into a corner because it wishes to savage at me, but because it wishes to keep me safe. My lion was keeping me safe because it loved me, and the man came and shot into it and killed it. Do you understand, Robert?"

"I think I do, Joseph," I said. "It's a matter of psychology the way you put it. Animal psychology. But you killed the man."

"I threw him away," Joseph said. "I was angry, and I did not know if he was going to shoot into my lion again, or into me perhaps. I was very angry."

"But you didn't mean to kill him, did you?"

"No," Joseph said.

I thought I had got something there. I saw Joseph's point of view perfectly. It was all a matter of interpretation. To you and to me and to George Gavin Gould that lion was a savage lion, about to do murder: to Joseph it was just his own friendly

Joseph pleaded Not Guilty, but there was no argument as to the facts. Joseph had assaulted George Gavin Gould. He had picked him up and thrown him against the bars of the cage, and as a result of this violence George Gavin Gould had died. The Defence called witnesses to prove that the deceased had been suffering from a disease called cardiac something, and the inference was that he had not taken a lot of killing. They put Joseph in the Box and asked him simple questions. They asked, "Did you wish to kill this man? Did you mean to kill this man? Did you know that you had killed this man?" And each time Joseph said, "No." The counsel for the Defence was not the one I had seen in the Solicitor's Chambers; the one I had seen then was only the Junior, this one was a middle-aged man; he looked a distinguished and capable lawyer and I think he was; he made it quite clear to me, and I hoped he had also made it clear to the Jury, that Joseph's action was unpremeditated, and that he had never had the slightest intention of killing.

"This is a case of manslaughter," he said. "And manslaughter only."

The question of Joseph's sanity was debated at length. Two alienists were called. One was on Joseph's side and one wasn't. The one who wasn't said that Joseph was suffering from a disease called "systematised ambitious paranoia," and that this meant that he was mad. The friendly one disagreed. He admitted that Joseph had a paranoic mental constitution, but he said that this was a common mental state, many sane people had it, and that all one could say about such people was that they showed a tendency to develop a systematised delusional insanity. "Compare this man's mental state to a soil," he said. "It is a soil which is prone to grow a particular weed, but I have found no sign that the weed has in fact grown in it."

The Judge was a little, birdlike man, and he thrust his face over the Bench and pecked impatiently at this alienist. "Your metaphors would no doubt be of interest to a Horticultural Society," he said. "But let us have the blunt facts in this Court. Is he responsible for his actions?"

"Yes, my lord."

"Then that is all we want to know," the Judge said. "He is sane."

It was all over by the forenoon of the second day. The jury, after retiring for only eleven minutes, returned a verdict of guilty of murder, with a recommendation for mercy; and the Judge, on passing sentence, declared that owing to the precarious state of the deceased's health he approved and endorsed the jury's recommendation, but was himself unable to give it effect.

"I sentence you, Joseph Hamilton," he said, "to be hanged by the neck until you are dead."

Joseph swallowed and leaned forward towards me. He opened his mouth, closed it again, and shook his head.

The policemen turned him unobtrusively and led him down the steps.

I watched the back of Joseph's head for what seemed a very long time, and when at last it disappeared from sight, I put my arms on the gallery rail and hid my face in my arms, and cried.

. . . . . .

Afterwards, I went to Jacobus's place. I had promised Lizzie that I would come straight to her with the verdict. I whistled at the foot of the backstairs, and Lizzie came down at a run, wiping her hands on her apron, her eyes hooked into mine.

"Well?" she said.

"Not so good, Lizzie," I said. I cleared my throat.

"Go on. Tell me," she said.

I am allowed to visit Joseph once a year and do so religiously. He has settled down to prison life. He is "on the land," as they say inside, and it is just the job for him. He has charge of two fine Suffolk mares, shares the responsibility for the pigs, and is hoping for the milk cows. He thinks there is a very good chance that he will get the milk cows when the cowman is discharged next year. He is still fond of birds and has a wide range of bird friends. It has become my duty to send him a sack of birdseed each month, and in return for this small service he has called his favourite raven Robert.

I couldn't ever bring myself to tell Joseph that Lizzie had married Rags Gorman. I was under the impression that Joseph thought that Lizzie was waiting for him and that the news would be a great shock to him, but I was as mistaken about this as I was about everything else, for I learned recently that the Gormans have been visiting Joseph each year since their marriage and that Rags has even promised to find him a job when he comes out.

I find it all very hard to understand.